The Shortest DISTANCE Between LOVE & Hate

Sandy Hall

Swoon READS

SWOON READS | NEW YORK

A SWOON READS BOOK
An imprint of Feiwel and Friends
and Macmillan Publishing Group, LLC
120 Broadway, New York, NY 10271

Our books may be purchased in bulk for promotional,
educational, or business use. Please contact your local
bookseller or the Macmillan Corporate and Premium Sales
Department at (800) 221-7945 ext. 5442 or by email
at MacmillanSpecialMarkets@macmillan.com.

Library of Congress Control Number: 2018955609
ISBN 978-1-250-11912-4 (hardcover)
ISBN 978-1-250-11911-7 (ebook)

Book design by Sophie Erb
First edition, 2019

1 3 5 7 9 10 8 6 4 2

swoonreads.com

For Shayla Flournoy.

Giver of ideas.

Receiver of complaints.

CHAPTER ONE

Record scratch.

Freeze frame.

Yup, that's me. Paisley Turner. Making out with a random guy at my first college party. You're probably wondering how I got into this situation.

Not that it really matters at the moment, seeing as how all I can think about is this guy's hand on my waist and his fingers in my hair and, oh my god, there's his tongue in my mouth.

WE HAVE TONGUE, PEOPLE.

This is the weirdest, most wonderful thing that has ever happened to me.

Should I be thinking so much?

I turn my brain to silent mode and concentrate on the kissing.

When that doesn't work, I take to cataloging the moment,

so I can remember it always. The way his fingers lightly brush my neck and send a chill down my spine. How the pulsing bass seems to beat along with my heart. The way the dark basement around us fades from existence. The slightly minty flavor on his lips that makes me wish I had brushed my teeth before leaving my dorm room.

But I wasn't thinking about making out when I left my dorm! I was thinking, *I've never had beer before, and I don't want the first time I taste it to be tainted by toothpaste breath.*

Is this how college is going to be? Walking into parties and being swept away in a kiss?

This was not in the brochure.

Did I even get a brochure?

Focus, Paisley!

All too soon he pulls away from me. I want to chase his lips with my own, but I realize I'm breathless and a bit dazed and could probably use a break. I look up at his face. He's so tall I want to climb him like a tree. Just scamper up him and perch on his shoulder and hang out there in his sandy-brown hair. But then I wouldn't be able to see his eyes, which are dark brown, at least in the dim light of the basement.

I am the whitest white person, there's no denying that, but my hand on his neck practically glows white because he's got this tan that's like something you'd see in a teen drama that takes place near the beach.

"That was . . . ," I say.

"Yeah," he responds when I don't finish my sentence.

I lean back and try to ignore the way the damp of the wall immediately seeps into my shirt.

"I could use a beer," Mystery Boy says. "You want a beer?"

I nod and almost as soon as he walks away, my new roommate, Stef, ambushes me.

"What the hell is going on?" she asks. Her voice isn't accusing, more intensely curious. Which I understand. This is a very curious situation.

"I don't know!" I stage-whisper, glancing over at The Boy. He's standing in the beer line, waiting for a new keg to be tapped. I turn my back to him because I don't want him to be able to read my lips. I start talking. Fast. I need to get this full story relayed before he comes back over.

"So, I'm standing here in the corner, playing with my phone, trying to talk myself out of begging you to leave early. Then that guy comes up to me and he was like, 'Remember me?' And I was like, 'Yeah, totally!' Because I didn't want to admit to not knowing him. I figure he's probably one of the guys who was in our group at the choosing-a-major thing earlier."

"Yeah, maybe. I don't remember him either," Stef says. "But I'm following you so far."

"But then! Then!" I say, gesturing wildly to emphasize how completely unexpected this situation is. "Then he's like, 'I've always wanted to kiss you.' And I was like, 'Huh?' But I didn't say 'Huh,' because honestly, all I could think about was that literally on the walk here we were talking about how I'd never kissed anyone and this was, like, too good to be true."

Stef is watching him, observing him. I can tell she's going to be a really good roommate. "I wish I could place him," she says. "We've been inseparable for the past three days. Maybe he was sitting behind us at the welcome convocation yesterday?"

"I don't know. But the thing is, who cares? He's a really good kisser, and I can play along."

She grins. "Well, I'm glad to hear he wasn't harassing you. When I looked over and saw this big dude all over you, I was worried for a minute. I was this close to interrupting." She holds her fingers a hair's width apart.

"I like and appreciate those instincts," I say.

"But then I saw your arms wrap around his neck, and you seemed relaxed and into it. This makes me think we should have a sign for a time when you aren't into it. Or when I'm not into it, for that matter."

I nod along even though what I'm really thinking about is kissing this boy some more right away.

"He's coming back over!" Stef says in a whisper yell. "Try to find out who he is! I'm going to talk to that girl over there, the one playing beer pong. You can't be the only one of us who gets to make out at our first college party."

She slides away just as The Boy returns with two red Solo cups of beer.

"Here," he says. He smiles a sort of tight-lipped smile that might not be attractive on most people, but on this guy, it really works.

"Thanks," I say.

He shuffles in place looking as awkward as I feel. Possibly even more awkward.

I wish we could go back to making out immediately. I

suppose we can't enjoy our beer and make out at the same time.

All I know is that I am not the same person I was when I walked into this damp, slightly gross basement a little over an hour ago.

"I like your T-shirt," he says, his cheeks pinking up. I might actually be in love with him. "Pilot episode," he reads out loud, gesturing toward my boobs. He quickly puts his hand down when he realizes where he's pointing.

I want nothing more than to assuage his embarrassment. That is my only goal.

"You should know that the way to my heart is through complimenting my T-shirts. I make them myself. I got really into screen printing a few months ago. It's like my hobby." Oh god, that's so unbelievably weird. Why did I say that?

"You're really into screen printing T-shirts?" he asks, a bemused expression crossing his features.

"It's a long story," I say.

"You'll have to make me one sometime."

"I could definitely do that." Okay, that's a little more like it. Maybe he's not totally turned off by my bizarre, nerdy hobby.

"So why 'pilot episode'?"

"Well, I figure if my life were a TV show, this party would be featured in the pilot episode."

He laughs.

"Though I have to say," I continue, "I feel like they really distort college parties on TV, unless this isn't a fair representation of one to begin with. I'm pretty sure we're currently being exposed to asbestos." I point up toward the world's saddest disco ball hanging from one of the exposed pipes.

"My roommate, Ray, his brother Luis lives here," The Boy explains even though I don't technically know who any of these people are. He gestures toward the corner where there are two boys with their heads bent over the keg, laughing about something; their dark hair is nearly black and their golden skin like something from a teen telenovela that takes place near the beach. I don't get a good look at their faces, but I can tell they're brothers even from across the room.

"That's how I got invited," he continues. "I have to admit this seems pretty spot-on to me."

"I must watch too many shows about rich kids," I say.

He laughs again. I'm beginning to really like his laugh.

-CARTER-

This is unbelievable! This is amazing! How is this even happening?

Paisley Turner is right here in front of me, chatting away, making me laugh, and acting like nothing happened five years ago. And we're bonding. At least I think we're bonding.

I saw her a couple of times in passing over the past few days. But we weren't in the same orientation group so I never got close enough to talk to her.

I'm not sure how I got up the nerve to tell her that I

always wanted to kiss her or why it was the second thing that came out of my mouth. I guess I'll blame the sip of vodka I had with Ray while we were pregaming in our room.

When Ray invited me to a party at his brother's house, I expected a dank, dim basement. That's how my older sister Thea always described college parties. I was prepared for that. I was not prepared for Paisley Turner to wander in.

She takes a sip from her cup and turns away for a minute, giving me the chance to really look at her. She hasn't changed much since eighth grade. Same brown hair, same short haircut, same inquisitive green eyes.

"So are you on the swim team?" I ask.

"No," she says. "But my roommate Stef is."

I nod and take a sip of beer. It's really not great.

She takes another sip and wrinkles her nose.

"Is this supposed to be good?" she asks.

"I was thinking the same thing! The way people go on and on about beer, I always expect more from it."

"Right? I've never tried it before and I was expecting much better." She pauses, shaking her head as she takes another sip. "This might be the worst thing I've ever tasted."

I twirl the liquid in my glass and sniff at it. "I'm detecting swamp water and something else. Something earthier," I say in a snobby tone.

She laughs. "It has a bouquet of skunk."

"Ah yes. Organic, I'm sure." I take another sip. "It's medium-bodied with a whisper of backwash."

"And the finish," she says. "The finish is something

heretofore unknown to me. Something like butts with a hint of ass."

We can't stop laughing now.

Somehow in the midst of this conversation, I've actually finished my beer.

I stare down at the empty cup. "I guess making fun of it makes it go down easier. Maybe that's the trick that no one tells you about."

She takes a last gulp from her cup. "Guess so," she says.

This time we go over to the keg together, little bursts of giggles bubbling up as we think of something new and funny to add.

"There really must be some kind of beer industry conspiracy. I don't know how so many people can like it when it tastes like this," I say, taking another gulp.

"We should really get to the bottom of this. Maybe start a podcast about the beer industry conspiracy."

"We need to start with beer industry propaganda."

"You mean, the commercials with the scantily clad women and the endless summer fun?" she asks.

"Exactly."

Anytime I think we're about to lose steam in this conversation, one of us says something else funny, insightful, or both. I'm not sure I've ever actually laughed this hard. Hours seem to pass like minutes. I've heard people use that phrase before but had never personally experienced it in real life.

"Okay, so aside from hating beer, what else do you hate?" I ask. I have a feeling anything that Paisley says is going to be enormously entertaining. "Like, what are your pet peeves?"

"Hmm," she says, eyes going wide. "I have so many, starting with people who walk more than two across on a sidewalk and won't get out of the way when you need to pass them. Also, when the fitted sheet comes off one corner of the bed, chewed pen caps, and people who use radar sounds for their cell phone ringtone."

"That's quite the list," I say.

"I could go on and on," she says. "What are yours?"

"I hate excuses," I say. "I hate people who make excuses and I hate making them myself." This is the truth, but I didn't expect to share such a serious truth at the moment. But might as well be up-front from the beginning.

"Wow. That's very specific and makes my pet peeves seem petty."

"Nah, I've just thought about this a lot."

"Obviously. And duly noted, I will never make excuses to you."

A yell erupts from the beer pong table.

"Dammit, Bart!" someone yells and I look over.

I glance at Paisley and she's looking at me. "What?" she asks.

"I thought I heard someone call my name."

"Oh, okay," she says, and giggles. I think she might be getting drunk.

On our third or fourth beer—I'm not sure because I'm definitely drunk at this point—Paisley takes a long sip and ends up with some froth on her nose. My life has become a god-damned romantic comedy tonight.

"You've got a little something," I say, pointing at my own nose.

She tries to brush it away and misses it, so of course I have no choice but to brush it away myself.

"Thanks," she says, her eyes lingering on mine.

This is the moment to kiss her again. This is the time to make my move. I don't want to be greedy but I want more.

As I'm about to lean in, a human blur runs past us toward the stairs and out the back door. Paisley pulls back and away from the moment.

"I think that was my roommate," she says.

"You think?" I ask, trying to get Paisley's focus back on me.

She stands. "I know it was my roommate."

Abandoning her empty cup, she runs up the stairs and out the back door in pursuit.

I figure I might as well follow. Couldn't hurt, might even be seen as chivalrous.

I find them in the corner of the tiny backyard. It's mostly full of garbage. College kids have no pride in a place. There's a perfectly good bicycle in the corner with two popped tires and a rusted chain.

Paisley's roommate is standing near that bicycle, bent at the waist with her hands on her knees, breathing heavily, her long, dark hair creating a curtain around her face.

"What's up?" I ask Paisley.

"Stef doesn't feel well, so I think we're going to head back to the dorm."

"What dorm do you live in?"

"Robinson."

"Oh, me too! I'll walk back with you."

We head out to the street, leaving the depressing back-yard behind, and Stef walks a few feet in front of us, sway-ing a little.

"I don't think she can really hold her alcohol," Paisley says.

"Oh right, yes, not like us."

"No, you and I are obviously seasoned drinkers." She lets out a loud belch and giggles.

"This is probably the most I've ever drank in one night," I admit.

"Same," she says. "I just feel so full." She rubs her stomach.

"Maybe this is why people do shots. So they don't feel so full," I suggest.

Stef stands at the corner waiting for the light to turn in our favor. There's not a lot of traffic out in the wee hours of the morning on the roads surrounding our campus, but it's good to know that even though she's drunk, she still remembers to follow the rules of the road.

"I am Estefania Gomez! And I am here to have fun!" she yells into the street.

"Sure you are, Stef!" Paisley calls back to her.

"I'm sorry I interrupted your time with the cute boy," Stef says over her shoulder as a lone car passes.

"I'm cute?" I ask Paisley.

"Don't be coy. You know you're cute."

"I really don't know that. It's nice to hear," I say, my neck heating up.

She gives me a sidelong glance and steps in front of me

to link arms with Stef as the walk sign lights up. I stay a few paces behind them, realizing that I probably should have told Ray I was leaving the party. We don't have each other's numbers yet, so I can't text him.

Hopefully he'll realize I left and come back to the dorm on his own. Or maybe he's staying at his brother's tonight. I don't know his life.

Either way, I doubt he'll be worrying about me. I make a mental note to exchange numbers with him tomorrow, though.

When we get to the dorm, Stef tries to use her card to get in, but she's holding it backward. She's basically the cartoon stereotype of a drunk person. Paisley helps her out and we enter the building. I stand and wait for the elevator with them.

"Um, so this was fun," I say.

"It really was," she says. Stef tugs on her arm, pulling her into the elevator.

"Good night," I say.

"Night, Bart," she says as the doors slide shut.

It takes me a second to process, and when I do, I almost hit the up button to stop the elevator.

"Did she just call me Bart?" I ask the empty hallway.

CHAPTER TWO

-PAISLEY-

I wake up with a smile on my face.

I don't think that has ever happened before, in my entire life. I can't imagine that it will ever happen again, so I hold onto the feeling. I honestly didn't know it was something I was capable of.

All thanks to The Boy.

Ah, The Boy. So cute, so silly, and he even walked Stef and me back to the dorm. Not that I believe we needed protection, but it's nice to feel like he cared enough to leave the party. Especially since I might be in love with him.

I shake my head because that thought is way too embarrassing. We just met. I am in lust with him. And even that might be too much. I don't really "do" emotions.

But we made out.

And it was *good*.

I can't stop calling him The Boy in my head, even

though I know his name is Bart. I roll it around but it doesn't really suit him.

"I see you smiling over there," Stef says.

I hadn't even noticed she was awake. She's sitting up in her bed, reading something on her phone. She's not looking at me but that doesn't keep me from blushing.

"Are you feeling better this morning?" I ask, hoping my embarrassing thoughts aren't written all over my face. I roll onto my side and realize that living with a roommate is going to be like a yearlong slumber party. Hopefully in a good way.

"I am," she says, putting down her phone and turning toward me. "I'm sorry I dragged you out of there, but I got claustrophobic. And I was so full. I definitely drank too much beer."

"Never apologize," I say. "I was happy to walk home with you."

"But you would have been happier walking home with your mystery man."

"We did walk home with him. And his name is Bart."

She smacks her forehead. "Wow. I seriously drank too much. It wasn't even like I felt that drunk."

"You were pretty drunk."

"I'm really sorry."

"No reason to apologize."

"He doesn't seem like a Bart," she says.

"I know."

"Well, he's a cutie no matter what his name is."

"I honestly can't believe any of that happened," I say,

my mind going back to that moment over and over again. He just walked up to me and asked to kiss me. Stuff like that doesn't happen to me. I suddenly can't wait another second to tell my high school friends.

I pick up my phone as Stef leaves the room to go to the bathroom.

But as I try to compose a text to Lizzie and Madison, I feel like I don't even know where to start. I feel so off from my usual self because of what happened last night. I feel like they won't even recognize me. They'll be like, "This isn't Paisley. Who stole her phone? Paisley, blink twice if you're in a hostage situation." And Henry! I can't fathom trying to explain this to Henry. Even though he's my best friend on earth, he'll judge me so hard.

Instead I go for something simpler, setting myself up for later so I have somewhere to talk about The Boy. Bart, I remind myself.

Paisley: I've decided we need a new group text now that we're away from each other. A sacred group text, one where we can come together and share our most sacred thoughts.

Madison: I concur.

Lizzie: Seconded.

Paisley: Motion passes.

Madison: Do we have anything to address yet?

Lizzie: I would like to propose that the Sacred Group Text (aka SGT) is not a place for eye rolling or disregarding of feelings.

Madison: LIZZIE, do you feel like we eye roll and disregard your feelings?

Lizzie: Not really. It was more of a disclaimer so I can say that I really miss my boyfriend even though he literally left for college yesterday. I'm eye rolling at myself for being like this.

Paisley: I withhold my eye roll.

Madison: I regard your feelings with the utmost respect.

Lizzie: Thanks, guys.

"So, what's on the agenda today?" Stef asks, breezing back into the room and throwing herself down onto her bed.

"Orientation stuff out the wazoo," I say. I glance back at my phone, trying to justify not telling Lizzie and Madison about The Boy. The time will come soon enough, and I'll be able to explain so much better once I get to know him better.

"Ah yes, the wazoo. People don't use that word nearly enough."

"Seriously. I guess I need to shower," I say.

"Yeah, same," she says, taking a sniff at her armpit and making a face.

I laugh.

We shower and brush our teeth and head out to the dining hall. We have another campus tour this morning and some kind of speech from someone about something and a barbecue tonight. I'm already so over tours and speeches.

I suppose I should enjoy it while it lasts seeing as how classes start soon enough and I have my first work-study shift in just two days.

I was really happy when my financial aid package included work study. Apparently, all the work-study jobs mostly involve managing desks and checking IDs while you get homework done, something I definitely need.

The only thing is, my work-study assignment ended up being the six to nine shift at the campus fitness center. That's six to nine IN THE MORNING. I'm exhausted just thinking about it.

Stef and I eat breakfast, taking our time choosing options at the omelet station.

"I can't believe they have an omelet station," I say.

"I hope they taste as good as they smell," she says.

The good news is that, yes, they do taste as good as they smell. And there is no bad news at breakfast.

I wake up to the beautiful sounds of Ray snoring.

He came in late last night and pretty drunk but didn't ask about where I went before he passed out.

I check my phone and try to convince myself not to call my sister Thea. I need to check on my mom, and normally, I'd just text. But it's too easy to hide reality in a text. I need to hear that everything is okay, not just read it.

I go out into the hall so I don't disturb Snoring Beauty.

"Hey, Thea," I say when she answers.

"Hey there, little brother. What's up?"

"I've been at college for almost three days, and I haven't heard from you or Mom. Therefore, I'm worried."

"There's nothing to worry about," she says, almost too fast.

"How can I know that for sure?" I ask, sliding down the wall outside my door and landing hard on my butt.

"Well, you can't know anything for sure," she says.

"Where's Mom right now?"

"She's out on the porch, drinking a cup of tea."

"It's not too cold for her?" I remember the good old days, where it felt like my mom was always worried about me. But things change fast when your mom gets diagnosed with breast cancer. A lot of plans changed and decisions were made. We sold our house in Delaware, and the two of us moved in with Thea in New Jersey. I'd already planned to go to college in New Jersey, to go to the same university Thea did, so this worked out really well.

"It's not. She's fine."

I sigh.

"Was that a sigh of relief or frustration?" she asks.

"Probably both."

"I understand."

"I need you to swear that you won't lie to me about stuff. I need to know that I can trust you. I know Mom will never tell me if she doesn't feel well, and I have enough guilt about being away."

It's Thea's turn to sigh. "Which is why you don't always need to know everything. We've been over this, Carter. Why would I add to your guilt? When I'm here and taking care of things? Let me be the adult."

"But—"

"But nothing. There's a reason you and Mom moved back here. It was so she could live with me and you could go to college. You're only an hour away. If I need you, I promise I'll let you know."

I squeeze my eyes shut and lean my head against the wall. I nod. Even though I know she can't see me.

"Listen, Carter. I love that you care. I love that you want to know what's happening with Mom. And I know that Mom loves that you care too. But I don't want to bug you with every little thing. With inconsequential things."

"Is there anything inconsequential about cancer?"

"No. But I need you to trust me. How can I make you trust me?"

"Will you text me every day?"

"Do you really want me to text you every day?"

"I want to know that everything is fine. You can literally

text me in the morning and be like, 'She's alive. Everything is fine.'"

"Okay," Thea says after a beat. "I can do that."

"But also, you know, tell the truth. 'She's alive. Things aren't fine, but there's no cause for concern.'"

"How about this? I'll text you when I get to work. Then you'll know everything is fine. If I'm at work, that means I know she can handle being alone most of the day. Or at least until the nurse comes for her infusion at lunchtime."

"That seems fair," I say, because it does.

"You have to promise you won't get pissed off at me if the texts wake you up every morning."

"Oh, don't you worry. I'll be up earlier than you will."

"Because you stayed up all night? I remember college, Carter. You can't fool me. I'm not that old."

"No, because I got my work-study assignment and I'm going to be working the early-morning opening shift at the fitness center three days a week at six a.m."

"Ew. Gross."

"Yup."

"That's a rough assignment. You should see the face I'm making right now. It's like I smelled something bad. Even I don't have to be at work until nine, and I have a real-life grown-up job."

I laugh. "I'll think of you fondly when I'm dragging my ass out of bed at five thirty in the morning. Or maybe five forty. Or five forty-five. My dorm is pretty centrally located. I'll have time to walk over to the fitness center and maximize my sleep. Hopefully. But no matter what, I'll think of you fondly."

"I'm sure you will."

"So you absolutely promise to keep me updated?"

"Do you absolutely promise not to get mad at spam messages?" she shoots back. She knows me too well.

"I will text 'STOP' if I want them to stop."

"Good. So tell me. How's everything so far? Let this twenty-four-year-old live vicariously through you."

"It's good. It's different than I expected. So far, orientation has been more like summer camp."

"How's your roommate?"

"I like him. He's got an older brother who goes here, so that helps. He's on the swim team, so we went to a party at his house last night. It was fun, but I don't really know why people like beer."

"Not liking beer isn't a bad thing."

"There's also this girl, Paisley," I say. Even just saying her name out loud makes me happy. "I went to middle school with her before Mom and I moved away, and I honestly can't believe she's here. I had such a crush on her."

Thea laughs. "That's a serious coincidence. Definitely keep me posted on that."

"I'm not sure if anything is really going to happen there."

"How come?"

Because nothing good ever happens to me, I want to say. But I don't want to go down that road with Thea. She'll just give me a pep talk about keeping my chin up and all that bullshit.

I'm not really that much of a defeatist; I just haven't been much of an optimist lately.

"I don't know," I say after a few more seconds. "Just a vibe? I didn't get her number. It was probably just a onetime thing."

"Who knows? Maybe the universe will help you out."

"Does the universe take requests?" I chuckle. "She didn't even seem to remember who I was. And she called me Bart."

"Bart?"

"Yeah, I think she misheard someone at the party."

She laughs again. "My advice? If you're interested?"

"Are you going to tell me to be myself?"

"Well, normally yes. But as I recall, middle school Carter was such an asshole, so maybe be better than yourself."

"I could be someone else entirely. I could be Bart."

She laughs. "But seriously. Next time you see her, say something about how you wanted to hang out, and if you had her number, you could text her. It's just testing the water. Very casual. If she rejects that, back off. If she doesn't, you can move forward."

"That's so smart."

"It's what I'd want a guy to do in this situation."

"I feel like I'm cheating on my gender," I say. "Like I'm getting secret tips."

"You are, Carter. You are."

When I finish my call with Thea, I go back in the room and Ray is awake.

"Hey," I say, remembering something he mentioned the other day during icebreakers with the rest of our floor mates. "Were you serious about being on the trivia team?"

He rolls his eyes and sits up. "I'm ready. Make fun of me. Luis never holds back, so I'm prepared."

"I'm not going to make fun of you," I say, sitting down on my bed. "Were you on your high school quiz team?"

"I was," he says. "Were you?"

"Nah. I was busy with other stuff, but it always looked fun."

"I was the *Jeopardy!* teen tournament champion last year," he says.

"What?" I ask.

"Yeah, I haven't mentioned that?"

"Um, no, definitely not," I say. "That's amazing!" If not also a little intimidating. Pretty sure that means Ray is a lot smarter than me. And definitely a lot more interesting.

-PAISLEY-

After a morning and early afternoon spent doing orientation things, and keeping my eyes peeled for Bart around every turn, Stef and I decide to go back to the dorm for some quiet time rather than going on a guided tour of the science building.

It's way too hot out for even one more guided tour.

By the time we get back to our room, I'm a sweaty mess.

"Who knew our dorm was on the opposite end of campus from the science building?" Stef asks, slightly out of breath.

"We do," I say. "We know that now."

"I'm so glad I'm not planning to major in anything sciencey."

We lounge on our beds and stare at the ceiling for a few minutes.

"What am I going to do?" I ask without any type of preamble.

"I don't know. How do people do this?" she asks, automatically knowing exactly what I'm talking about.

I flip onto my stomach. "I need to find him. I'm pretty sure he lives on the first floor, and everyone has their names on their doors right now. So we could just go down there and look around."

Stef taps her finger to her lips. "This is like Cinderella minus the glass slipper."

"He's my Cinderfella," I say with a cheesy grin.

She shakes her head but starts to laugh anyway.

"I must find my Cinderfella!" I say in a high-pitched falsetto.

"Please, ma'am, have you seen this boy?" Stef whips out her phone and pulls up his picture.

"When did you take this?" I ask, grabbing her phone and holding it close to my face, like I can glean some further information from it. Also, he might be even cuter than I thought.

"I just got lucky at one point. The crowd parted and I got a really clear view of him. It seemed like something that you might appreciate."

I laugh. "Send that to me. I need to examine it. Maybe he has a tattoo of his last name somewhere on his person."

We spend the next several minutes examining Stef's paparazzi photo of The Boy, but that doesn't get us anywhere.

My phone rings in my hand and I yelp with fright.

"It's just my mom," I say.

"I'll go get us some brain food from the vending machine," Stef says, leaving the room.

"Hey, Mom," I say, answering the phone.

"Hey, sweetheart. How are you?"

I smile. "I'm excellent."

"Good."

"How are you? Are you lonely yet?"

"Not yet, but I'm sure I will be soon." It's just been Mom and me for pretty much my whole life. We lived with her parents for a while, but mostly it's been the two of us. Leaving for college was . . . emotional. No matter how much I hate to admit it.

"Make sure to drink things besides beer and energy drinks." This is her way of trying to be extra mom-ish. It's kind of adorable.

"When have I ever had an energy drink?"

"I don't know. That just seems like something kids these days would drink for pulling all-nighters or whatever."

"Well, the good news is that classes haven't started yet, so I don't have any homework or exams and therefore don't have to pull an all-nighter."

"So relieved," she says. "Anyway, I wanted to hear your voice before I knew you got busy with classes. I hope I didn't interrupt anything."

"Nah," I say. I almost tell her about The Boy, but it feels too new, too ephemeral to talk about with my mom. I'll tell her. Eventually. It's the same with telling my friends from home. I'm not ready yet. "Just chatting with my roommate, Stef."

"You like her?"

"I do."

"Are you lying?"

"I'm not," I say with a smile.

"I had to ask just in case she was in the room."

"I understand. You're very covert. I feel like you've learned a lot from all those cop shows that you watch."

"I really have learned so much. Someday maybe I'll be a detective."

"Good luck with that," I say. Missing her comes over me so quickly that it makes my eyes sting and my throat close. For a second, I can't swallow.

"Well, I won't keep you, like I said, I just wanted to hear your voice."

"Thanks, Mom."

I hang up with her a minute later, and Stef comes back in the room, tossing me a bag of French Onion Sun Chips.

"How did you know these were my favorite?" I ask.

"I might be a little bit psychic," Stef says. "About snack food."

I laugh.

We while away the rest of the afternoon and then get ready to go to a carnival off campus. It's not part of orientation week, but according to everyone we talked to, the whole school goes to it.

I'm sure Bart will be there, and all my questions will be answered.

CHAPTER THREE

-CARTER-

The big carnival that everyone is going to tonight is a solid twenty-minute walk off campus. Apparently, they're trying to make it look like the boardwalk at the Jersey Shore, but it's not really working. Especially since we're actually in New Jersey and I'd guess 95 percent of the people at this thing know exactly what the boardwalk looks like. And it does not look like this super generic carnival.

Ray and I arrive together, and I keep my eyes peeled for Paisley.

"You're going to tell her who you are, right?" he asks. I explained the whole situation to Ray on our walk over here.

"Of course," I say, even though I'm lying. After talking to Thea this morning, I can't help but think maybe she was onto something. Maybe it's okay not to be myself, just this once. At least for a little while. It's not like I purposefully introduced myself to her as someone else. She just misheard and made assumptions.

"But are you *really* going to tell her?" he asks, eyeing me like he could just hear every word of my thought process. "You look kind of sick to your stomach."

"I just want a chance to make a better second impression. Middle school Carter was kind of an asshole, as my older sister put it so delicately. But I just want to show her I've changed."

"By being someone else?" He puts his hand on my shoulder. "This is a terrible idea."

"I need to at least try."

He drops his hand and shakes his head at me. "Well, she's right over there," he says, gesturing.

I turn and find her and her roommate wandering through the carnival games. Paisley looks completely adorable, as usual. She's wearing a T-shirt that says NOW WHAT?

"Are you coming with me?" I ask Ray.

"I think I'd rather be pretty much anywhere else."

He walks fast to catch up with some of the other people from our floor and doesn't look back.

Maybe I should feel bad, but this is such an incredible opportunity. When do you ever really get a second chance to make a first impression? Never.

Paisley catches sight of me then and waves.

I wave back and jog over, unable to keep a smile off my face.

"Hey, Bart," she says. "I'm Paisley, by the way. I can't remember if I actually mentioned that last night."

"Hey, Paisley," I say, grinning. "I kept hoping our groups would run into each other today."

"Same," she says. "But I'm really happy to see you now."

She twists her hands together in front of her and blushes. I can tell she really means it, and that only solidifies my decision to keep letting her think I'm someone I'm not. It's not my best plan ever, but it's not my worst. Just for a little while longer. I'll tell her later. Like maybe I'll take her on the Ferris wheel, and when we're at the top and there's nowhere else to go, I'll confess. She'll have to sit and listen to me for as long as it takes for the ride to end. She'll understand.

Stef leans and waves in my face. "Hey there," she says.

"Oh hey, hi," I say, coming back to reality.

"Well, I'm going to let you guys get to it," Stef says, awkwardly clapping her hands together, before wandering off.

"She could stay and hang out with us," I say to Paisley.

"I know. I don't think she really wants to. I'm sure she'll run into someone she knows soon enough. I'm pretty sure the entire swim team is here."

I nod. We smile at each other a little too long.

"So," she says, gesturing around us. "This is quite the spectacle."

"That would be one way to describe it," I say.

We're jostled by a group of people, so we move out of the way.

"Are you from around here?" she asks.

I should probably stay away from any and all details about my life, but I'm pretty sure I can answer this one without adding to my lies. "Nah, I'm from Delaware."

She nods.

"All my high school friends go to University of Delaware," I continue. "And they started orientation last weekend. So I feel . . ." I pause, looking for the right phrase.

"Out of step with them already?" she offers.

I nod. "Exactly that."

"All of my friends are scattered at home and other colleges, but I can imagine if they were all in the same place, it would feel weird."

"It does. I figure I'll see them when I can, but I'm going to make new friends." I chew my lip. "Seems like I already have."

"Maybe even more than friends," she says, with an adorable little head tilt.

"Seems like it, maybe," I agree.

I can't stop smiling.

"So, where should we start?" she asks.

-PAISLEY-

We wander around for a few minutes, looking at the food trucks and the game booths and the ride offerings. It's a really good carnival and I can see why the student body attends en masse.

"Let's get something to eat," Bart says.

"Definitely." I inhale deeply. "I love funnel cake. I wish funnel cake was a regular offering at each and every meal. I hate that it's so limited in availability."

"Weirdly, they used to sell these mini funnel cakes in my high school cafeteria."

"Were they any good?" I ask.

"There were pretty decent. Because let's be real, as long as the cake is hot and fried and they put the powdered sugar on at the right second, there's no such thing as a bad funnel cake."

We get in line for food at the taco truck and Bart pays. I let him. I really don't know what I've become. Letting a boy buy me dinner. Usually I'd be all like I MUST PAY FOR MYSELF. But it's kind of like, if he wants to do nice things for me, it makes me feel nice.

I hate myself.

But I like HIM so much.

We grab the end of a picnic table just as the group who was sitting there leaves. I take a sip of my drink and look around.

"I can't believe school starts the day after tomorrow. I'm totally not ready," he says.

"I know," I say.

"I'm taking a history class with a professor that everyone really likes, though. I was talking to people about her at the party last night, and when I told them I had history with Professor Brightly, they all said she's the best."

"Cool." I file that information away for later. "I definitely haven't studied my schedule closely enough to remember any of my professors' names."

"Oh, well this one stuck out because her name is Henrietta Brightly. She sounded like she should teach at Hogwarts."

I laugh.

As we throw away our garbage after eating, Bart grabs my hand.

I can barely think about anything else. I can only concentrate on the way his fingers feel intertwined with mine. Now I understand why people walked all over high school like this. I always thought holding hands seemed arbitrary and unnecessary, like what's the point. But I get it. It's special. It feels good.

"So, I feel like if we're really going to lean into this whole carnival thing, I should win you a teddy bear or something," he says.

I balk at this. I haven't completely lost my sense of self. "Or I could win you something."

"Or we could compete and see who's best at something." He waggles his eyebrows at me.

"All right. I like that idea."

"What's your game?" he asks.

"Well, usually I'm better at arcade stuff—claw machine, Skee-Ball, that kind of stuff. But I don't see any of that around here. What about you?"

"I'm pretty good with a basketball throw or maybe that balloon game?" he says, gesturing.

"I like darts," I say. "Pointy things sound like the way to go." I tug his hand in that direction and he follows.

I'm definitely sad to have to drop his hand when it's our turn.

He goes first. He misses initially, but then hits the next two, winning me a medium-sized prize. I pick a zebra because it's a little bit cooler than your average stuffed animal.

"I shall name her Debra. Debra the Zebra," I say, pronouncing *zebra* with a short *e* so it rhymes with *Debra*.

When it's my turn, I pop three balloons and get a bonus dart, so I pop another.

He's impressed, so I channel Elle Woods from *Legally Blonde*. "What, like it's hard?"

He selects a giant unicorn. I can't stop laughing.

"It's so fluffy!" he yells in a silly voice.

With our winnings in tow, we continue to wander until we decide it's popcorn time. After buying a bucket, my treat, we find an empty bench near the rides and sit down to people watch.

I crunch on a handful of popcorn, while Bart pretends to feed his unicorn.

"What are you going to name her?" I ask.

"It's a her? How do you know?" he asks, examining the toy. "Is there a certain way to tell male and female unicorns apart?"

"Obviously, all unicorns are women because they are perfect and wonderful," I explain.

"Oh right, right," he says, and then laughs. "So what do you think I should name her?"

"I don't know. That's up to you."

"I think I'll call her . . . Hula."

"Hula? Like the hoop?"

"And the dance. She just looks like a Hula to me."

I laugh. "I'm really glad we have more to talk about than just beer."

"Me too."

"I think it's about ride time," I say. "But first! A trip to the bathroom."

-CARTER-

While Paisley runs to the bathroom, I eat more popcorn and check my phone. I have three texts from Ray.

> **Ray:** I can see you two across the carnival. I'm not stalking you. I swear.

> **Ray:** But I can tell that you haven't told her yet. It's pretty obvious from the way you're talking and laughing.

> **Ray:** And I just don't think this is cool. I don't want to be that guy. And I hope you won't hate me for saying so, but you need to set this straight.

Rather than responding to him, I turn my phone off. I know this isn't the best idea. But like I promised myself earlier, I'll tell her on the Ferris wheel.

When Paisley returns, she's ready to roll.

"But what do we do with the kids?" I ask, holding Hula and Debra.

She bursts out laughing. "I think the kids can handle riding with us."

The ride operators at the tilt-a-whirl and scrambler won't let us take our prizes on, but there are no such rules at the Ferris wheel.

Paisley holds both of them in her lap.

We get to the top and have to wait for people to get on. It's now or never. I need to tell Paisley the truth. My hands are sweating so I wipe them on my shorts.

"So," I say. I have to get as much of it out as I can before we get to the bottom of the ride again. Before she can leave me. "I'm really nervous, but I want to say—"

Paisley interrupts. "I know what you're going to say, and I just want you to know that I'm in. I like you too."

"You do?" I ask, shocked.

"I do." She licks her lips and the ride starts moving again. She puts her hand over the unicorn's eyes and she kisses me briefly, softly.

"Is that okay?" she asks.

"That's amazing. That's unbelievable. That's incredible," I say. Before I can babble more, she starts kissing me again and she doesn't stop until the ride stops. We're both dizzy and dazed, from the height, from the ride, from the kiss.

As we walk back to the dorm, hand in hand, Paisley keeps up a line of chatter but I have trouble focusing. I'm just so happy that she likes me. It's like all my dreams are coming true.

When we get to the elevators, she pushes the up arrow.

"So when can I see you again? Should we exchange numbers?" This question makes me panic; there's something about her putting me in her phone under the wrong name that makes me feel totally wrong. Like that's a line I can't cross.

"This is so silly," I say, shaking my head. "But my phone's

dead, and I got a new number and I don't know it by heart yet."

She giggles. "That is silly," she says.

"But let's meet tomorrow?" I say. The elevator dings.

"There's more orientation stuff tomorrow."

"I know, but there's also the first-year barbecue tomorrow night. Let's meet there at six?" I say as the doors open.

She kisses my cheek. "I can't wait."

-PAISLEY-

I step in the elevator and I stare at him as the doors close.

As soon as the elevator's moving, I start dancing and twirling around in the small space.

I can't believe what an amazing night I had.

When I get into my room, Stef is still out. I shoot her a text that's all exclamation marks and happy face emojis. I consider getting in the shower, but instead I just lie down on my bed and think about Bart. About kissing him, about holding hands.

I should be embarrassed, but instead, I just feel . . . happy. Completely, totally, genuinely happy.

I roll over and grab my laptop. I open up the scheduling website and search for a history class with Professor Brightly. There's only one available for freshmen; every other one of her classes requires a prerequisite, so this must be the class that Bart is in. Before I can overthink it, I click on the class and change my schedule, dropping the anthropology class that I was originally assigned.

It's not like I know what I want to major in. During the placement testing, I was advised to take a wide range of courses this year to figure out what I like and what I don't like.

I like history. I might as well take a history class.

It's just a bonus that Bart's in the same one.

A wonderful, amazing bonus.

I float on a cloud all the next day. I desperately want to see Bart, but he's nowhere to be found. Not at the activity fair, or the library tour, or the ice cream social.

Thank goodness we made plans to meet up at the barbecue.

After the longest day ever, it's finally almost time to go.

"You ready?" Stef asks.

"I was born ready," I say. We'd stopped back at our room after our last orientation event ended to change into jeans and freshen up. I even put on some mascara.

Before we walk out the door, I text the selfie Bart and I took the night before to Lizzie and Madison along with the statement "I think I'm in love" and then I turn my phone to silent.

I look forward to seeing what they have to say later on.

I can't wait.

CHAPTER FOUR

-CARTER-

The welcome barbecue is being held on the field inside the track near the fitness center. I time the walk over there and adjust my alarm settings accordingly. It'll take me about seven minutes to get to work in the morning.

As soon as I see Paisley, all thoughts of my 5:38 a.m. wake-up time are forgotten. I make a beeline for her while Ray holds a spot for us at the end of the very long food line. He hasn't said anything else to me about confessing to Paisley. He hasn't said much of anything at all.

Paisley and her roommate are busily filling plates. Neither of them notices me until I'm right next to them. Stef nearly drops her plate when she sees me.

"Good lord," she says. "Make some noise or something."

"I just wanted to say hi," I say. "So, hi."

Paisley turns around and grins at me, her eyes glittering in the early evening light. I can't believe how cute she is.

"I like your T-shirt," I say before she even says hi back.

It's a simple white shirt that says "sup," all lowercase, in a fancy navy font across it.

"I figure it'll start the small talk for me," she says. "But I have to admit. I didn't make this one."

"I appreciate your honesty," I say. "I'm going to get in line with my roommate, but I'll find you when I'm done."

She nods and I walk away, looking over my shoulder a few times, just to smile at her again. This is ridiculous. I am ridiculous.

When I slide into the line next to Ray, no one behind us protests. Maybe people care less about cutting in college.

"I swear the entire freshmen class is here," Ray says.

"It's really crowded," I agree.

"How do you even go about planning something like this?" he asks.

I only hum in response, because the logistics of a barbecue for thousands of people is not in my wheelhouse. I can't quite work up the interest in it. The line moves at a crawl.

"Did you tell her?" Ray asks, his voice serious.

"Soon, I swear." He just shakes his head.

When he's done filling his plate, he stalks off without a word.

I search the crowd for Paisley, and I spot her and Stef sitting along the fence. I walk over, totally forgetting about Ray.

"Hey there," I say, taking the empty seat next to Paisley.

"Hi there," she says.

"Ho there," Stef says, staring at me from Paisley's other side.

I nod and smile, but I really only have eyes for Paisley.

"How was your day?" I ask.

"It was good," she says. "Kind of boring. Sad I didn't see you around." She shoves the rest of her hamburger in her mouth and that reminds me that I have food of my own to eat. I take a bite and look away. We don't need to watch each other chew.

She and Stef make small talk for a minute or two, and then Stef excuses herself to go hang out with some of the other first-year members of the swim team. We smile at each other. Things feel more awkward tonight, but that's definitely my fault.

"Ah!" Paisley says. "I forgot chips."

"I'll go get a plate of them for us to share because I didn't grab any either," I say. I take a deep breath while I wait in line and give myself a pep talk. I need to come clean. I need to tell her that my name isn't Bart. She might be annoyed, or maybe even embarrassed, or hate me for lying to her, but I can't let this go on indefinitely.

I feel ready to confess.

When I get back, she's staring at her phone. She looks up at me, and I know my plan has gone horribly wrong.

"Who are you? Tell me your name," she says, her tone accusing, her whole demeanor changed in the minutes I was away getting chips. She's leaning away from me and looking intently at my face, trying to read my expression. "Your real name."

"Carter Schmitt," I say, along with what I hope is my most charming smile.

"You can't be serious."

I open my mouth to say something, anything, but she shakes her head and jumps up, leaving me in the dust.

-PAISLEY-

I run all the way back to the dorm. It's only as I go to enter the building that I realize I don't have my wallet, where my student ID is, which is what I need to use to get in the front door of the dorm.

I touch my room key in my pocket, but my ID card is definitely on my desk. I should probably get one of those phone cases with the card slots so I never leave my dorm without it.

I debate going back to find Stef, or at least text her, but then Carter is right there and I suppose I have no choice but to talk to him. Apparently, he can't take a hint. Running away from him wasn't enough.

He doesn't say a word. I purse my lips at him dramatically and turn away. There's a picnic table right outside the door to our dorm, so I take a seat on one of the benches and Carter sits next to me.

I stand up and walk around the table, taking the seat across from him instead. I want to see his face while I tell him exactly what I think of him. I am almost shaking with anger. I couldn't believe when I took out my phone and saw the responses I'd gotten to the picture I'd sent Madison and

Lizzie. Madison asked who the guy in the picture was because he looked familiar.

But Lizzie. Lizzie knew immediately.

Lizzie: That's Carter Schmitt. Didn't you used to hate him?

He was indeed Carter Schmitt and I did indeed hate him. We went to middle school with him, but then he moved away before high school.

I clasp my hands together and grind my teeth. I suck in a deep breath.

"I'm so pissed off now that I know who you are."

He studies me, squinting at the setting sun, but doesn't say a word.

"You lied to me."

"Technically—"

I cut him off. "You can shove that technicality right up your ass."

He holds his hands up defensively. "You acted like you knew me at the party."

"I thought I'd met you earlier in the day. Not because I thought I knew you from middle school! I didn't recognize you. I think I blocked you out because you were so hateful."

"Ah, right," he says, leaning back and crossing his arms. "Um. Well. What does this mean in terms of us?"

I can tell he's picking his words very carefully. I can't believe I didn't recognize him. I guess I didn't spend much time looking at him in middle school. I always regretted not defending Henry more, but anytime Carter got on his case it was almost always when Henry was alone. Makes sense. That's how bullies tend to work.

"Us?" I ask. "You were hideous to my best friend. And you've been lying to me from minute one."

"I didn't lie to you. I wanted to make a new first impression."

I hold out my hand in a "stop" gesture. "Sorry. There's no excuse for some of the stuff you did to Henry. And there's no excuse for lying to me. Also, I thought you hated excuses." I make sure my tone is extra mocking on that last word.

"I do," he says. "But it's not an excuse. It's a fact."

He has obviously never dealt with someone who knows how to hold a grudge. He's about to find out how much I care about his "facts."

"You flushed his clothes down the toilet during gym class. You hid his glasses so he had to walk around in his sports goggles all day. You copied his homework and cheated off of him during tests. You stole his lunch. You didn't even eat it. You would take it and stomp on it and make a mess and leave the remains in the hallway for the custodians to clean up."

I'm rattling off the things I remember. There was probably a lot more, stuff that Henry never told me or that I never heard about.

"You remember all that, huh?" Carter asks.

"Of course I do. And so does Henry."

"So you probably had an I Hate Carter Schmitt Club."

"We called you Farter Shit, but yes. Basically."

"Clever. I can't believe the whole school didn't call me that."

"Well, I was the only one who called you that, mostly to make Henry laugh. And since I'm not a horrible person, I never spread it around school."

He gulps. He knows I'm right.

"This does not look great for me." His face is bright red, like he has the worst sunburn that I've ever seen.

"It doesn't," I say. I'm glad he seems resigned to this, that he's not fighting me, even though I'm kind of in the mood for a fight.

"Well, I'm sorry. Whatever good that does at this point."

"It's a little late for sorry."

He wipes his hands down his face and sighs. "Can we at least be friends?"

"I don't think so."

"We live in the same dorm, we're at the same school. Wouldn't it be easier to be friends than enemies?"

"No. I'll avoid the crap out of you. Don't worry. This won't affect your life at all."

"Jeez, Paisley, that's not what I'm worried about."

I hate how my name sounds coming from his mouth. I honestly don't know the last time I was this angry. It probably involved Amelia Vaughn, queen bee of my high school class. Carter and Amelia would be perfect for each other.

"I liked you," I say, my voice teetering too close to tears. I need to get away from him. Especially because *like* barely covers how I feel about him. How I felt about him. At least he proved he wasn't worth it sooner rather than later.

I stand and stumble over a large rock, stubbing my toe. That was super smooth. I march toward the door, ignoring the pain in my toe and the lump in my throat.

Of course, when I get to the door, I remember again that I left my room without my wallet, so now I get to wait for either someone to let me in or for Carter to notice and help me.

I want to throw up.

Carter sits at the picnic table with his head in his hands, like he might cry. He better not cry. He doesn't deserve to cry.

He looks up then and meets my eyes. I put my hands on my hips and stare at the door, willing it to open.

I hear him shuffle across the path over to the door, and he slides his ID card through the reader.

"Thanks," I say.

"The least I can do," he mutters.

He doesn't come into the building with me and I don't look back. I run up the six flights of stairs to my room and text Stef.

> **Paisley:** Don't leave the BBQ on my account, but when you get home have I got a story for you.

I add a few angry emojis for emphasis before hitting send.

I know I should text Henry, but I'm not prepared to text

Henry. Or anyone else from high school. I have betrayed myself and everything I stand for by making out with Carter Schmitt. I really thought I was falling for him. I can't be trusted.

Stef comes in a few minutes later. "What's up? I need to know right now."

I suck in a deep breath.

"It's bad news. Very bad news."

-CARTER-

Well, that went poorly.

At least I know that if I run from the fitness center to my dorm, it only takes four and a half minutes.

I go to my room and lay down on my bed, putting my hands over my face. I honestly can't imagine a worse turn of events than what just happened.

The door to my room opens and Ray comes in.

"Did you tell her?" he asks.

"Well, she found out."

"That's weak, dude," he says, shaking his head. "I don't know what you were thinking."

I shrug. "I wasn't really."

"Did you apologize?"

"She didn't want to hear it."

"I feel like that's just the worst excuse. You didn't have to get yourself wrapped up in this in the first place. So not cool. Not a good look for you."

"Listen," I say, sitting up and scrubbing my hands across my face. "I'm not usually like this. I just made a mistake."

"Sure, whatever you gotta tell yourself. I'm going to my brother's tonight. He lives closer to my first class tomorrow anyway."

"Yeah, okay."

"Later," Ray says.

Great. The girl of my dreams hates me and my roommate can't stand to be around me and I have to be up for work before the sun rises. Everything is just perfect.

-PAISLEY-

"So," I start. I slide down to the floor and lean against my bed. Stef sits next to me. "His name is not Bart. His real name is Carter Schmitt."

"I like it. Carter Schmitt."

"I hate it. I hate him."

"What the hell happened at that barbecue? I left you alone for thirty seconds. What could he have possibly done in such a short amount of time?"

"Well, I found out that he lied about who he was."

"Yeah, that's not cool."

"On top of that, we went to middle school together. And he was really mean to my best friend, Henry. I sent a couple of my friends a selfie Carter and I took last night, and one of them recognized him right away."

"Friends are so useful like that."

"They are." I sigh. "I can't believe how mean he used to be to Henry. I swear I blocked it out."

"Sometimes boys are mean," Stef says.

"This was above and beyond thirteen-year-old-boy mean. Carter made sure Henry's life was miserable. Like, I don't even really want to go into it."

"How did you not recognize him?" Stef asks.

"Well, he moved away before high school. And he looks different now. Taller, better haircut. No braces. And in a dark basement? I didn't recognize him. I don't know why I didn't put two and two together after that when I saw him when I was sober and in better light. But I guess I didn't think I knew him. I don't know. I can't explain it. Maybe I was protecting myself."

"An ignorance-is-bliss scenario."

"Exactly."

"Were you and Henry ever together?" she asks.

"No. Definitely not. I told you we went to the prom as friends. Nothing else."

"And you never had a crush on him?"

"Henry?" I ask with a laugh. "It never even went through my head to have a crush on Henry. People in high school always assumed we were together but we're friends. Really good friends. It's kind of annoying how you can't be best friends with a guy without it being suspect in some way."

Stef nods. "Sorry. I just want to get the story straight, you know?"

"Yeah, I suppose these are all important details for someone coming into this later in the game."

"Exactly."

I put my head in my hands and sigh.

"I can't believe he lied to me like that."

Stef rubs my back and I feel a little better.

"So what are you going to do?" she asks.

I shake my head. "What can I do? I need to dodge him for the next four years."

"You don't want to confront him?"

"I kind of did confront him. He followed me back from the barbecue and we had a fight outside."

"He seemed so nice."

"Well, he's not. He obviously hasn't changed since we were thirteen if he's pulling crap like this."

"Yeah," Stef agrees.

"I'm just really sad," I say. "I thought he liked me. I really liked him. I thought this was going to lead to something. The whole thing didn't even last forty-eight hours. It's like I'm not even allowed to be happy that long." I hate how whiny I sound, but I also feel like I need to get it out of my system.

"We need to think of a distraction."

"Yeah, good idea."

"You could make an angry T-shirt to wear tomorrow, and that way, if you see him, you can point at it and he'll know to stay away."

I laugh. "I like that idea."

"Now we just need to come up with the perfect saying for it."

I decide to compose a lengthy text to Lizzie and Madison, explaining what's been going on with me for the past forty-eight hours.

But Henry. How am I ever going to tell Henry?

I frown at the thought. Telling Henry is not something I'm prepared to do at the moment. I'll leave that to Future Paisley. She can handle that I'm sure.

For now, I respond to the texts from Lizzie and Madison and brainstorm angry T-shirt slogans with Stef.

It's exactly the kind of catharsis that I need.

CHAPTER FIVE

-CARTER-

In the midst of everything that happened yesterday, I almost forgot that I have my first day of work today. Luckily, I remembered to set up an alarm for it before everything went down. I knew that I would forget that I needed to be up at 5:38 in the morning.

It's just the kind of thing I would block out of my mind.

I know myself.

Especially after what happened with Paisley yesterday.

Man, did she lay into me. And I deserved it, but that doesn't mean it didn't hurt.

This week is on-the-job training, but I still have to be there at six to learn how to open the building up for six thirty. Who in their right mind goes to the gym at six thirty? (I know. I know. Lots of people. But that's hard for me to fathom. I'm not judging them.)

I barely slept last night because I kept hearing Paisley's

list of the things I did to Henry. It repeated over and over again. You would have thought it might lull me to sleep eventually, but instead it was like each time I went through the list, I remembered things in more vivid detail. I was such an asshole back then. I could and should apologize for that stuff, but not to Paisley. I should apologize to Henry. This isn't exactly her battle to fight.

I just don't know what to do about the way I acted the past few days. I don't know how to make that up to her. Because it's something I did *to* her. No matter how I justified it in my head.

It's not cold out, but I shiver on my walk to work. I'm probably in some kind of shock from lack of sleep. At least I don't have to operate heavy machinery.

There's another person lurking around the front doors of the building when I get there, but I can only just make out their shadow in the predawn light. I check my phone. It's 5:58. I can't believe I made it.

And that's when I realize who the other person at the door is. For a second, I think it must be a mirage.

But no. It's Paisley.

It's really Paisley. Has she come to continue our argument at my place of employment?

"Well, if it isn't Farter Shit," she says. Her eyes are droopy but at least she has a thermos of coffee with her. She takes a sip. I envy her. All the thoughts and arguments I had with myself in the middle of the night immediately go out of my head.

"Morning, Parsley," I say. People calling her Parsley in

middle school was another thing that came back to me last night. As soon as it's out of my mouth, I know it's not the best way to show her that I've changed. But I can't take it back now.

She rolls her eyes and I prepare another zinger. But it's too early in the morning to get into a war of words right now.

"What are you doing here?" I ask instead.

"Here? At the fitness center? At six in the morning?"

"Yeah."

She just shakes her head. Guess I'm supposed to assume she works here too.

It's now 5:59. How can time possibly be moving this slowly?

Before I can say anything else, or even think of anything else to say, the door opens and our boss Jordan lets us in. She wastes no time showing us where to store our belongings and giving us the rundown of the rules. When Paisley takes off her hoodie, I notice she's wearing a T-shirt that says I DON'T HOLD GRUDGES, I JUST REMEMBER FACTS.

She doesn't look at me.

"You can have that coffee with you at the desk, along with water. I know it's early in the morning. Technically the rule is only water at the desk, but I definitely make exceptions for the openers. And the closers. It can be a long day, and we're here until eleven most nights," Jordan says.

Paisley and I nod. She looks more awake than I feel.

"And you," Jordan says, turning to me. "If you want coffee, we do have a machine in the office. Feel free to brew some when you get in. I already have a pot going this morning." I've never been a coffee person, but I'm starting to think that this job will make me one.

Our training continues at a brisk pace. Jordan is going to stay with us during our shifts for the next week to make sure we get the hang of everything. She also hands us checklists of what needs to get done before opening and a handbook on employee conduct. She's remarkably efficient. And obviously a morning person.

Jordan goes to take a phone call and leaves us alone at the desk just after eight o'clock. I think I should be able to manage checking someone in, but I'm worried about anything bigger than that. It's a good thing we have a full week of training ahead of us.

I watch Paisley rearrange the area of desk right in front of her. She stacks the event pamphlets and organizes the pens and pencils into a neat bouquet in the container.

"So, are you scheduled for lots of opening shifts?" I ask when I can't take the silence for one more second.

She doesn't respond.

"Are you doing work study?"

Nothing.

"Are you ready for classes to start?"

Still zero. I thought maybe trying a different tack would surprise her out of her silence.

"You can't ignore me forever," I say, just as Jordan reappears to show us how to enter basketball court reservations into the system.

When our shift is finally over, Paisley disappears so at

least we don't end up walking in the same direction together in awkward silence.

And now I'm imagining something worse than an awkward silence, an awkward distance. Where to avoid walking with me, she remains ten paces behind me, or even crosses the street so that we don't have to be near each other.

I don't know how to deal with being hated.

I walk to the dining hall to waste some time before my class at ten, but I barely taste my breakfast.

-PAISLEY-

This is the worst morning ever. It's like my emotions are playing tug-of-war. I really *liked* him. I don't like people often, but I really liked Carter. At least, I did when I thought he was Bart.

And now to have him show up where I work? Knowing I'll have to see him all the time? It makes my stomach twist in knots.

I'm very careful to stagger my exit with Carter's. I know I saw Pop-Tarts in the vending machine in the staff room, and they'll make a perfectly serviceable breakfast on my way to class. Later on, I'll get lunch and eat something healthy, I promise myself.

While I'm in the staff room, I look over the shift schedule that Jordan gave us earlier, and of course I'm on here three days a week and every other Saturday morning with Carter for the foreseeable future.

I suck in a deep breath. I'm going to have to steel myself toward him. Because unfortunately, he does have a certain kind of charm that I'm apparently susceptible to. I'm going to have to nip that in the bud.

As I walk toward the quad where my first class is, I ponder the phrase *nip it in the bud* because it's better than thinking about Carter. I find an empty bench outside the English building to eat my Pop-Tarts and drink the coffee that I picked up at the student center along the way.

I decide to text Henry. Even if I don't tell him about Carter, I should check in on him, see how things are going. That's what a good friend would do.

Paisley: Hey.

Henry: Hey yourself.

Paisley: How's . . . everything?

Henry: Well. It's fine. Mostly. My room-mate seems fine, but it's been a lot of icebreakers and group activities. I need more alone time.

Paisley: I'm sure you'll get used to it soon.

Henry: Yeah, I know. It's an adjustment

period. I can't judge the whole experience from the past few days.

Paisley: Exactly.

Henry: Is there a reason for this im-
promptu text session?

Paisley: Can't a girl just text her best
friend on a random Monday morning?

Henry: Of course a girl can. But you're
putting off a weird vibe.

Paisley: How can you get a weird vibe
via text message?

Henry: I like to think I know you,
Paisley. And I can't help feeling like
something is up.

Paisley: Nothing is up. Aside from me.
But I've been up for hours thanks to my
work-study assignment.

Henry: Oh right! The early-morning shift.
No wonder I was getting a weird vibe.
You're a morning person, but not an ASS
CRACK OF DAWN morning person.

Paisley: Really, who is?

Henry: Besides my mother and people on sitcoms who meet up with their friends for breakfast before they go to work?

Paisley: Yes, besides that.

Henry: No one. Absolutely no one.

Paisley: So, am I allowed to ask about the "A word"?

Henry: Aardvark? Andromeda? Asshole?

Paisley: ANXIETY.

Henry: Oh that. I'm fine. I feel fine. Seeing a therapist this summer helped a lot. Taking medication is helping. I need to set up an appointment with someone on or near campus, but like. In general, I feel fine. Good.

Paisley: Thank you for that update. Am I allowed to inquire about this regularly or is it an off-limits topic?

Henry: I don't know. Do we really need

to talk about it? Haven't we talked about it enough?

Paisley: Sure. That's why I asked. But you know I'm here if you need to talk.

Henry: Yes, Paisley. I'm well aware. And thank you.

Paisley: You're welcome.

Henry: Good talk.

Paisley: Yes. Well, it's almost time for my first class. CALCULUS. Tell me you're proud of me.

Henry: I'm so proud of you.

Paisley: I'll talk to you later! Have a good first day of class.

Henry: You too. I'm on my way to calc too. But it's calc for engineers and I'm worried I'm not ready for this.

Paisley: You are the champion of calculus. Don't you even worry your pretty little head about it, buckaroo.

I know he's standing somewhere laughing. Henry loves it when I say stuff like that.

I try my best not to feel guilty about not telling him about Carter. I couldn't bring myself to do it. Henry is going to be so nervous all day today; I don't want to bring anything up that might make him feel worse. I don't usually tiptoe around Henry, but there's just something about this Carter situation that makes me want to hide it from him.

Probably my raging case of guilt and feeling like I betrayed Henry.

But I will tell him. Eventually.

I finish my breakfast and throw away my garbage. I stow my travel mug in my bag and make sure my phone is on airplane mode. I don't want anything interrupting or ruining my first college class. This is why I'm here. To get a good education. It's not about work study or Carter or even making friends. It's about learning.

I take a seat in the second row, toward the windows. It feels like the right seat for me. I want to do better in college than I ever did in high school. And I feel like the key to that is not letting myself slide into the back row.

There's still ten minutes until class starts and I regret not staying outside in the sunshine a little longer, but now there are more people trickling in so at least I can people watch.

The back door of the classroom swings open and I glance back.

"Unbelievable," I mutter to myself.

Carter Schmitt (ew) freezes in the doorway when he sees me. The person behind him walks right into him and curses.

"Shit, dude. You can't stop like that."

Carter clears his throat and steps out of the way. "Sorry about that."

"Whatever," the guy says.

Carter shakes his head and slumps into the very back corner seat. For some reason, that feels like a win for me.

Class starts and I do my best not to think about Carter in the back. He doesn't have any effect on me; he doesn't matter. That's my new motto. So what if we have classes together and work together and live in the same dorm? None of that matters.

The universe isn't trying to tell me something.

Why would the universe be talking to me anyway? Doesn't it have more important things to do?

I have two classes in a row this morning and then another one this afternoon. Which isn't bad. I'm taking five classes this fall, even though they recommended taking only four your first semester. But I don't want to end up in summer classes. I want to get my money's worth out of the school year and have time to make more money during the summer. Not sit in a classroom four mornings a week. I suppose I could take online classes if I had to, but even that would be a time suck.

I take the same seat in my next class. Or the sameish seat. It's a large lecture hall for General Psychology, so the second row is a lot bigger. And wouldn't you know it, Carter walks into this room too.

Why me?

Why now?

I wish I could text Henry a whole string of expletives

and angry emojis. He's the only person who's really going to get how terrible Carter is. But that would require having the guts to actually tell Henry about Carter.

For lunch, rather than risking seeing Carter at the dining hall or even at the student center, I head to the basement of the psych building. There's supposedly a small convenience store down there.

I find it easily and get an apple and peanut butter crackers and a Coke. It's not the healthiest, but I'm starving and I don't know what else to do.

I swear that I'll eat a better dinner. I'm already imagining a plateful of french fries as I lurk outside my final class of the day, Early American History with Professor Brightly. And I know for a fact Carter will be in this one. Since, you know, I stalked him into it, a detail he hopefully won't notice.

I take a peek through the window in the door. The classroom is apparently empty the period before mine so maybe I can hang out in here for the next hour. I test the doorknob and jackpot! It's unlocked. The classroom is medium-sized, so I find the same approximate seat in the second row again and crack open my bottle of Coke. I flip through my psych textbook, while crunching on my apple.

Then, Carter walks in.

Not only does Carter walk in. He's carrying a bag of takeout from the student center and there are definitely french fries involved. My weakness.

My stomach makes the loudest rumble. It would probably show up on the Richter scale.

"A little hungry, Parsley?" Carter asks.

I want to shoot back something brilliant, really put him in his place, but my stomach answers with another grumble of starvation. It's hard to be clever when I'm this hungry.

He walks up to me, pulls a half-empty sleeve of fries from the bag and hands them to me.

"Seriously?" I say.

He shrugs as he walks back to his preferred corner seat.

I hold up a fry to the afternoon light pouring through the window. "Did you do something to this? Should I not eat it?"

He doesn't respond, and I'm way too hungry to worry about why he's being nice to me.

I will accept this gift. But in the future, I will be more prepared foodwise. It'd be too easy to fall into his trap, I just know. I must prepare for a long semester of seeing way too much of Carter Schmitt.

It would help if he wasn't so goddamned adorable.

CHAPTER SIX

-CARTER-

The first week goes by with Paisley ducking me at every turn. I had hoped that my french fries would act as a peace offering. I guess life doesn't work that way.

We only end up having three classes together, which is really three too many, but there's not much I can do about it. I consider switching around my class schedule, but it fits well with my work hours and I have the exact courses that I want.

It's Paisley's issue, not mine. She can switch if she wants to. Not to mention that I'm 99 percent sure that she switched into my history class after I told her about it. So that's her problem.

She shows up every day we're scheduled to work and to each of our classes. I see her once in a while in the dorm or at the dining hall, but she gives me a wide berth and I do the same for her.

We're both on the schedule for Saturday at nine thirty. The building opens at ten. That gives me a whole half hour to at least try.

I show up with coffee for her, even though she usually brings her own. But I figure maybe she'll need extra this morning. Maybe she went to a party last night and is hungover today. I feel this inexplicable need to make her like me. Or at least make her not hate me so much. I hope that coffee is the way to her heart.

She accepts the cup as I unlock the doors. The late summer sun is almost blinding as it bounces off the windows that span the front of the gym. I notice that for once she's not wearing a T-shirt with an aggressive slogan directed at me.

"You really didn't have to get me this," she says as she takes a sip. Her voice is froggy. She probably did go out last night.

"I just wanted to show you that I could do nice things. That I'm not the same kid I was in middle school," I say as we get started on the opening procedures. She nods and walks over to the bathrooms and locker rooms to unlock them, so I don't get to say anything more then.

The gym is busier than I would have expected that morning, but around noon it slows for a few minutes.

"So," I start. "How was your first week of school?"

"Listen," she says. "Making out with you was basically the biggest mistake I have ever made. But the universe is obviously forcing us to be together at every turn. I really hope that we can grow past it and pretend to be strangers who just happen to work together and see each other all the time. We don't have to be friends."

Wow, so that's a gut punch. She really knows how to throw them.

I don't know how to answer her.

She takes out her calculus textbook and gets to work on the problem sets we're supposed to hand in next week. I do not understand calculus. I should have stuck with some kind of easier math.

A few people come in and I check their IDs, giving them directions or answering questions. Paisley keeps working.

I can't stop thinking about kissing her.

Especially that kiss on the Ferris wheel. It was a whopper of a kiss. Full of electricity and chemistry. The kind of thing you usually only hear about in movies.

I need to come to terms with the fact that Paisley and I aren't destined to be together.

-PAISLEY-

I am so annoyed by Carter being adorable and bringing me coffee that I have no choice but to ignore him completely for the duration of our shift.

At some point while we're sitting side by side at the fitness center front desk, Carter gets up to grab something from the office.

I notice there's a screw loose on the backrest of his chair. Just hanging on by a thread. My initial instinct is to find a screwdriver and fix it. I mean, that could end up being my chair tomorrow. The chairs in here are always being switched around.

But this also might be a great moment for a tiny bit of revenge. For my own brand of justice. It's nothing that will hurt him, but maybe make him look and feel like a fool. Would that be so bad?

So I pull the screw and drop it on the floor.

I am an evil genius.

Carter comes back a moment later, plops down in his chair, and the back immediately falls off. He flails for a second but rights himself easily.

"What the hell?" he asks, but it's a rhetorical question and definitely not aimed in my direction.

But it feels good. This small act of Paisley-branded justice is exactly what I needed. It's a good balance.

"Oh dear," I say, acting like I only just noticed he was there. "What happened?"

"Chair is falling apart," he mutters. He picks up the screw and examines it, his eyes never coming to rest on me. I might as well be a houseplant.

"Terrible," I say.

He walks off in search of a screwdriver.

Let the games begin.

Paisley 1, Carter 0.

-CARTER-

Thea: Everything is fine.

Carter: I don't believe you.

Thea: Why don't you believe me?

Carter: Because no one ever starts a good news text message with "everything is fine." That phrase is a disclaimer used to make the receiver feel better when they hear whatever comes after it. Usually a "but."

Thea: What are you talking about?

Carter: Everything is fine, but . . . That's how that sentence usually goes.

Thea: Ah yes.

Carter: And also you said you'd text me from work every morning and it's currently ten o'clock on Sunday night. So you'll see how this is already leaving me suspicious of your intentions.

Thea: College is really teaching you some wonderful and new deductive-reasoning skills.

Carter: As much as I love our witty repartee, I need to know why you're texting.

Thea: And vocabulary! Look at you, using the word "repartee" correctly! So proud of you, baby brother.

Carter: Thea. You're killing me.

Thea: Everything is fine, but Mom has a fever. I wanted to tell you, not to make you worried, but so that you'll trust me to let you know when something is going on.

Carter: I'm calling you.

Thea: Don't! I don't want Mom to hear us talking about this. I just wanted to update you.

Carter: What are you going to do?

Thea: I called her nurse who said to give her something to take the fever down, that it's probably nothing to worry about, but that if it doesn't come down in the next forty-eight hours to bring her to the emergency room.

Carter: Just bring her now. Why wait?

Thea: For about eight million reasons.

Carter: Such as?

Thea: The hospital is full of germs and she could catch something else, something worse, than what she might have. It's probably a small cold, but with her immune system annihilated thanks to the chemo, her body overcompensates.

Carter: What's she doing now?

Thea: Napping in front of the TV.

Carter: Why is she napping at ten o'clock at night? Shouldn't she be in bed?

Thea: Fine. Napping is the wrong word. She dozed off watching something on PBS so I decided this was a good moment to text you. She pays too much attention to the details and what I'm doing. I didn't want her to realize that I was texting you because she would yell at me for making you nervous.

Carter: I'm already nervous! I'm less nervous when I know what's going on.

Thea: I know. Which is why I texted you in the first place.

Carter: You promise to text me when things get worse?

Thea: IF things get worse. Don't use WHEN.

Carter: Things getting worse just feels inevitable. Like we can only be so lucky for so long.

Thea: We were lucky. We'll be lucky again.

Carter: I'm glad you can be so optimistic.

Thea: How's school?

Carter: School is fine. It's still early in the semester but everything is fine.

Thea: I noticed you haven't mentioned that girl again. Is it because you feel weird talking about this stuff with your sister?

Carter: No. It's because nothing good is

happening with the girl. Paisley. She hates me.

Thea: What did you do to her?

Carter: Well, that's sort of the problem, it's not what I did to her, so much as what I did to her best friend. In middle school. And then I kind of, sort of, lied about who I was for a couple of days. It was all a misunderstanding!

Thea: Hmm. Sure. Sounds kind of suspect to me.

Carter: Maybe it kind of was. It definitely was.

Thea: So what are you going to do?

Carter: What can I do? I obviously offended her so badly that I can't make it up to her.

Thea: Good.

Carter: Good?

Thea: Yeah, you don't want to be THAT

guy, Carter. The one who chases after a girl after she's told you to stop.

Carter: I'm nodding. You just can't see me.

Thea: Good boy.

Carter: Do you think I can make one more try? Before I give up forever? Maybe she needed a cooling-off period.

Thea: Sure, but be ready to back off if she tells you to back off. And just . . . be nice. Go with your gut instincts. Don't go with the first thing that pops into your head. Count to ten and walk away.

Carter: Yeah. Good. Thanks, Thea.

Thea: You're welcome, Carter.

Carter: AND YOU BETTER KEEP ME UPDATED ABOUT MOM.

Thea: I WILL. I PROMISE.

Carter: CROSS YOUR HEART AND HOPE TO DIE?

Thea: STICK A NEEDLE IN MY EYE.

On Sunday night, Stef and I are at the dining hall with a group of people from our floor, but at the moment it's just the two of us getting drinks.

"What are you doing next weekend?" Stef asks. "A bunch of us from the swim team are going to Great Adventure."

"Ugh. I wish. I have no money."

"Bummer," she says.

"I know. All of my work-study money goes into an account I can't touch from the ATM so I'm a little cash-flow poor. I won't mind it when I have money for next semester, but it's annoying to work all week and have nothing to show for it."

We walked in at the same time as Carter and a bunch of guys from his floor, so now I have the added fun of avoiding him at the dining hall.

"How are things going with that?" Stef asks, casting her eyes in the direction of the salad bar where Carter can't seem to master the use of the small tongs for getting cherry tomatoes.

"Horrible."

"Have you considered changing your schedule?" Stef asks before taking a bite of her salad.

"I have but nothing works. Everything creates a domino effect." I refrain from telling her that at least one of the classes we have together is my fault. It's just too embarrassing.

I pause to get more napkins. As I turn around to go join the rest of our floor mates, Carter materializes next to me.

"Fancy meeting you here," he says with a smirk.

I roll my eyes in response and grumble to myself the whole way to the table. I stew silently as everyone else talks and eats around me. I need to stop letting him ruin my college experience.

On our way back to the dorm, Stef and I walk a few steps behind everyone else.

"I love your shirt," a girl says to me as she passes.

I have to look down to remind myself what shirt I'm wearing. It's actually an old one I made over the summer because of an inside joke I have with Henry. "Be your own sugar daddy," it says.

"Thanks," I say.

"It's cute," Stef says. "And funny."

"Is it? I just threw it on because it was clean."

When we get back to the dorm, I decide it's time to tell Henry about Carter. I've put it off long enough, but it's becoming apparent that Carter is going to be a fixture in my life and Henry is the only person who's truly going to appreciate how terrible that is.

Stef leaves to go study with some friends from the swim team, and I know it's the perfect time for me to text Henry.

Paisley: You busy?

Henry: Only a normal amount. What's up?

Paisley: I have something horrible to confess.

Henry: I'm terrified and curious.

Paisley: I made out with Carter Schmitt.

Henry: From middle school?

Paisley: Yes. How can I ever make this up to you?

Henry: There's nothing to make up to me? When did you make out with him? In middle school? You're just deciding to tell me now?

Paisley: No, Henry. He goes to college with me. And I met him at a party and I didn't remember him.

Henry: Paisley. It's not a big deal.

Paisley: I just want you to know how sorry I am. I feel like I've betrayed you and myself. I believed I was a most loyal friend only to go to college and make out with your archnemesis.

Henry: He was never my archnemesis. I'm not Batman.

Paisley: No, Henry. You're Superman and he's Lex Luthor.

Henry: No, Paisley. He was a middle school bully. It's nothing that dramatic.

Paisley: All right. You're right. I just really do feel bad. And like I need to bathe in Listerine.

Henry: Do you like him?

Paisley: No, he's terrible.

Henry: Then why did you make out with him?

Paisley: Because he was being nice.

Henry: So maybe he's not terrible anymore.

Paisley: Oh, hell no, I'm not letting him off the hook that easily. There's more to the whole thing. Like, I thought his name was Bart because of this thing that happened at the party. So, like, I kept calling him Bart and he DIDN'T CORRECT ME. He just let me go on with it. And then we hung out at this carnival and we kissed again and he won me a zebra and it was all just so fake. He lied to me! And I liked him!

Henry: Oh. Yeah. That's not cool.

Paisley: I know. He's clearly still the worst. Hasn't changed even a little.

Henry: I don't want you to feel bad on my account.

Paisley: Well, for the record, my loyalty is with you. Even if he hadn't been a lying bastard, I wouldn't be friends with him due to the principle of the thing.

Henry: And because you like to hold grudges.

Paisley: And that. So, how's everything going with you?

Henry: You don't have to change the subject.

Paisley: I could use the distraction.

Henry: Honestly, everything is good. I really like my classes and my roommate is good and I feel good.

Paisley: That's great. ☺

Henry: Or at least it's good. Since I used the word three times in my last text.

Paisley: Good is . . . good.

Henry: And at least I didn't make out with Farter Shit.

Paisley: See? Your glass is definitely half full. Do you have any advice?

Henry: Ignore him.

Paisley: Gee, I never would have thought of that.

Henry: Advice is what you ask for when you already know the answer.

Paisley: All right, smarty-pants. Thanks for being so cool about this, Henry.

Henry: You're welcome, of course.

CHAPTER SEVEN

-CARTER-

It's the start of our fourth week of classes, and Paisley is still avoiding me. Acting like I don't exist. I don't want it to bother me, and yet it does.

Barring when she's forced to speak to me at work, she hasn't said two words to me.

I try to keep in mind what Thea said. About being a good guy and giving Paisley some space. But it's hard. It makes me whiny.

Not to mention that it's driving me stark raving mad. I can't stop thinking about how well we got along with each other during those two glorious days before she learned who I am. I acknowledge the fact that I lied to her. I purposefully let her believe I was someone else. I understand why she's pissed about that.

It just seems sort of unreasonable for her to still be mad at me about something that happened in middle school. Isn't there some kind of statute of limitations on bad behavior? Isn't it time to move along? I think it is. Which is why I decide to try to talk to Paisley about what's going on between us. Since obviously she'll never broach the topic.

It's a quiet Saturday morning at the gym. We just opened, and it's the weekend of the fall festival on campus so there will likely be fewer people in and out. She's wearing a T-shirt that says LET THE GAMES BEGIN. As if I didn't already know this whole thing was all a game to her.

"Can we talk?" I ask her. This is it. This is my last run at being civil with her. I have to try. I'll never forgive myself if I don't try one more time. The idea of someone hating me makes me itch. Not to mention that I got myself all psyched up for this conversation and I'm ready.

She has her history book open on the desk and is diligently staring at it. I can't say she's diligently working because she hasn't opened a notebook or picked up a pen or even turned a page. I can only say she's doing her best to train her eyes on it.

"Honestly, Carter, I don't think the workplace is an appropriate location for this type of personal discussion."

"How do you know it's personal?"

She gives me a look.

I accept what she's saying and also, at that moment, like ten people all come in needing their IDs checked and to borrow equipment and to ask a million questions. So it's not the best time to talk anyway. But I can't help feeling sort of deflated. I promise myself I'll try again.

On Monday, when we're walking out of our history class, I can feel the opportunity in the air.

"Maybe now we could talk?" I say to her as we walk down the hall.

We don't have psych for twenty minutes, and I know she usually only goes to the vending machine for a quick snack. Not like she has big plans for this break.

"I don't think the classroom is an appropriate location for this personal discussion," she repeats again. Apparently, she likes this phrase. Why is it the more that she frustrates me the more I want to kiss her?

"Come on, Paisley. Can we please talk? We could go outside and talk. We have time."

She massages her forehead like I'm giving her a headache but she follows me out.

We take a seat on a bench. It's late September but feels more like August. Fall in New Jersey can be weird.

"So, what is it?" she asks. She pulls out her "Nevertheless She Persisted" refillable water bottle and takes a long sip, looking anywhere but at me.

"I hate knowing that someone hates me," I say.

"Well, I'm sure lots of people hate you, Carter. I'm not sure there's anything you can really do about that."

"I'm not talking about them." I wave my hand broadly at all my haters, hoping to make her laugh. I know she was probably trying to get under my skin with that comment, but she's not going to. I'm staying on task here.

"Are you talking about someone specific then?" she asks, picking invisible lint off her jeans.

This purposefully obtuse routine will get old quick, but I don't know what else to do beside push through it.

I will not let her get a rise out of me.

I will not let her get a rise out of me.

I will not let her get a rise out of me.

I repeat that phrase in my head for a few seconds. It feels good.

"Well? Someone specific? Something you specifically wanted to discuss? We have to be in class in fourteen minutes now. We don't have all day."

"I hate knowing you hate me."

She shrugs. "I hate knowing you were mean to my best friend."

"So, you and Henry are still friends?"

"Yes."

"That's good."

"He's a loyal and wonderful friend. I honestly couldn't ask for much better."

"And you guys never dated?"

"I hate that question more than I hate you. So now I hate you even more."

"Isn't *hate* an awfully strong word?"

"Maybe, but it's succinct and it gets the job done. I don't need a thesaurus to explain how I feel about you."

I chew my lip.

"Is there a point to all this?" she asks.

"Well, is there something that I can do to make you hate me less? I just want to be friends. We're obviously stuck with each other for the semester and more likely the whole year, at least at work. I don't want you to have a terrible time just because I'm here."

"Don't worry, I'm not having a terrible time. You're barely even a blip to me."

"But isn't there anything I could do?" I ask. I feel like I'm begging now. "Maybe we could form a truce?"

"If I think of something, I'll let you know, but I doubt it," she adds before I have a second to get my hopes up. Then she stands, hefts her bag higher onto her shoulder, and walks into the classroom building without another word.

I'm left on the bench feeling worse than I did before.

I'm pretty sure even the squirrels pity me.

-PAISLEY-

I'm not going to lie, Carter's plea for a truce was sort of endearing in an annoying kind of way. He looked so sad, and for a split second, I remembered how I felt about him at the top of the Ferris wheel. But then I crushed those feelings down and remembered my rage. Maybe if he hadn't deceived me the way he did. Maybe if he'd just been himself. Maybe I could have gotten over the middle school stuff.

But we'll never know now.

I don't want to be friends with him. I never want to be anything remotely like friends with him. But I might be interested in getting a little more revenge.

I say something along those lines to Stef the next day and she nods.

"I think I get that. But is a biblical revenge what you want? Like an eye for an eye kind of thing?"

"Yeah, minus the part where I flush his clothes down the toilet or steal his lunch. Or commit identity fraud."

"It's good to know that you're truly above some actions. Is that really considered identity fraud?"

I shrug. "I don't know, but that's what I'm calling it."

The first small prank presents itself a few days later. And "prank" is really overstating the situation, but I don't know what else to call it. Maybe "minor sabotage." Or maybe it's best to think of it as my own brand of Paisley justice, much like pulling the screw out of his chair.

I'm righting wrongs and bringing balance back to the universe, making life a little harder for him, the way he made life a little harder for Henry. Especially since I know Henry would have never stood up for himself like this.

Anyway, Carter needs to leave a half hour early one day because he has to go to office hours for some class, I don't know which one, and I wasn't paying attention. He tells me he'll stay a half hour later the next day and that if anyone should look for him, to just let them know. He already discussed it with Jordan and she gave her okay. I don't really answer him because, you know, I'm ignoring him.

Eventually he leaves and I spend the rest of my time pretending to make an outline for the writing assignment that's due next week when really I'm napping with my eyes open.

Moments before my shift is over, the director of the fitness center comes through and asks why I'm working the desk alone.

All I can see is an opportunity. It's time to throw Carter under the bus.

I shrug. "I don't know. My desk partner just left early."

"He didn't tell you where he was going?"

"No, he didn't say a word to me. If I wasn't sitting by the door, I might not have even known he left."

"Honest to god," the older man grumbles. "Kids these days."

I wish I could think of something else to say but he walks off before I can think of anything worthwhile.

Being bad feels really good. Perhaps mischief is my muse.

I practically bounce toward the dining hall when I meet Stef for lunch later that afternoon.

I fill her in on what happened at work.

"Don't go overboard," she warns. "You don't want to get in trouble while trying to get Carter in trouble."

"But he deserves it."

"I'm not saying he doesn't," she says with a shrug. "I'm just saying that you should tread lightly with these pranks."

"I prefer minor sabotage to the word *prank*. Or, if you prefer, vigilante justice."

"Of course. Right. You're a professional. Pranks are for amateurs."

"I'm so glad you get me," I say as we put our trays on the conveyor belt and leave for our afternoon classes.

"I know what you're going to say, but I have to ask," she says as we leave.

"What?" I wait for her to ask me an annoying question about Carter that has an obvious answer that's supposed to make me rethink my plans to destroy him.

"We're going out for dinner tonight, a couple of swim team people. Want to come?"

"Oh," I say, momentarily surprised and pleased that she's not harping on me about Carter. "Ugh. I wish."

"We need to figure out a way for you to make extra money."

"Yeah," I agree. "I need to be more liquid."

I take Stef's words to heart, both about making more money and being less intense about getting revenge on Carter. I decide to take it down a notch, even though Carter seems to leave himself open to these things. It's like he wants me to commit acts of minor sabotage.

The next time we work together he doesn't even seem to notice that anything is amiss. Maybe Jordan didn't even mention it to him. Maybe the big boss didn't make a stink.

But then Jordan comes out and says, "Carter, I need to see you for a moment in the office."

I wait ten seconds until I know they're inside, and then I slip down the hall quietly to eavesdrop.

"Why didn't you tell Paisley you needed to go to office hours?" Jordan asks.

"I thought I did!" he says. "I stood by the desk and—" He pauses. "Or maybe I didn't. Maybe I thought I did. Or maybe she didn't hear me. I'll be more careful next time."

"We're flexible here, but we definitely work on a 'three strikes and you're out' policy."

"Obviously, it's a fitness center," Carter says.

Jordan chuckles. How dare he make her chuckle while he's getting in trouble?

"I like you, Carter," she says. "But this is your first strike. If Mr. Martell hadn't found out about it, it wouldn't be a big deal, but I have to make it one. Especially since we had to fire someone yesterday for never being where they were supposed to be. Mind you, they were a lifeguard, so literally lives were on the line."

"I get it," Carter says.

"I'm going to be working on a new policy list, updating people on what's expected of them. Just follow the rules and everything will be fine."

"I get it. And I'm sorry."

Jordan says something else, but I can tell they're wrapping up. I nearly bust my ass racing back down the hall to make sure I'm at the desk when he returns.

"Any problems?" I ask when he sits down a minute later.

"Not at all," he says.

"It sounded like something was going down."

"Mm, yeah, it's definitely none of your business."

Interesting. He's avoiding confrontation. Maybe he's finally learned his lesson.

-CARTER-

Today is a bad day.

All days are kind of bad days lately, but today it was extra bad. Paisley totally threw me under the bus at work and now I have a strike on my record. I wanted to argue with Jordan but I knew it wouldn't get me anywhere. It seemed silly to make excuses. And it's only one strike.

It'd be really nice to have one good day, though.

I walk back from work alone, eat dinner alone, and go to the library alone.

I'm alone, of course, in my room later on, trying to

work on calc homework and getting nowhere. I'm going to have to suck it up and hit the campus tutoring center sooner rather than later. Calculus is not my forte.

Ray comes in, cracking jokes and in a better mood than I've ever seen him. Things have been rocky between us since I ditched him twice the first weekend of school, but maybe he's finally thawing out.

"Hey," Ray says, sitting down on his bed and going through his backpack. "Any chance you want to join the trivia team? We just lost a member and I remember you saying you might be into it."

I stare down at my calc book. I would love to join the trivia team. It'd be like getting a whole group of friends in one quick swipe, but there's no way I have time.

I shake my head. "Nah, there's no way I can do that."

"Why, because you're so cool?" Ray says.

I hold up my hands in defense. "No, it's because I feel overwhelmed by my schoolwork and work study and life in general." Things with Ray have been pretty cold since the first weekend of school. I'm not surprised that this is how he's reacting.

"Your life in general doesn't seem all that overwhelming."

"Well, since you never asked about my life in general, how would you know?"

Ray nods. "Fair. What's up with your life in general?"

I cough nervously. "I'm not, like, looking for your pity or anything. It's just my mom has cancer and—"

"Say no more," Ray interrupts. "I get it. You need to be available."

"Exactly."

"Sorry I jumped on you like that."

I shrug. "It's fine."

It's not really fine, but I honestly don't feel like talking about this for even one more second.

"How are things with Paisley?" he asks. It's definitely meant to be an olive branch, and I accept it.

"They're complete and utter shit."

"I'm not saying you don't deserve it, because you do, but I'm sorry that it still sucks."

"Thanks, man," I say, coloring in the margin of my notebook.

"You want to come hang out at my brother's? Nothing is really going on there tonight, but you know, could be more fun than sitting here and working on your calc homework or whatever."

"So, so tempting. And I hope you won't take it personally, but I gotta stay home and work on my calc homework. Problems to solve, scholarships to keep, miles to go before I sleep. That kind of business."

"Did you mean to rhyme that?" Ray asks, squinting at me.

"Not even a little."

We bust out laughing and I can tell that things are finally on the upswing with Ray. I never wanted to get on his bad side.

He leaves a second later, and I feel better.

Making up with Ray takes this a few steps up from the worst day ever.

CHAPTER EIGHT

-PAISLEY-

Paisley: I'd like to call this meeting of the Sacred Group Text to order.

Lizzie: Reporting for duty.

Madison: Yup, I'm here too. What's up?

Paisley: I need to make Carter Schmitt's life miserable. The suggestion box is officially open.

Madison: Something involving finger-nails? Pulling them out? Sticking things under them?

Lizzie: Paper cuts. Lots and lots of paper cuts.

Henry: PAISLEY. WHY.

Paisley: HENRY.

Madison: HENRY.

Lizzie: HENRY. Hello. I didn't notice you were even in this group text.

Henry: Hello, Lizzie. Yes. I am here.

Paisley: I decided to add Henry. I hope nobody minds.

Madison: I don't mind.

Lizzie: Welcome to the Sacred Group Text, Henry.

Paisley: So, seriously. I need to come up with some kind of revenge. I've recently taken to little bursts of Paisley justice. I pulled a screw out of his chair and the back fell off. I got him a strike at work by feigning ignorance. I feel like a whole new woman today, knowing that his life is a little more miserable thanks to me.

Madison: I understand. I don't condone purposeful violence, but I enjoy what you're doing.

Lizzie: Mm. Yes.

Henry: Please stop.

Madison: Stop what, Henry? The texts or the revenge plot?

Henry: Well. Not the texts. I like being in your group texts. It's always a good time.

Lizzie: We are super funny. I'm glad you enjoy being included.

Henry: What I don't like is the idea of Paisley exacting revenge in my name. Like, it could seriously blow up in your face.

Paisley: I just want to make him a teeny, tiny, eeny, weeny bit miserable. Is that too much to ask?

Madison: No.

Lizzie: Nope.

Henry: YES.

Paisley: HENRY.

Madison: HENRY.

Lizzie: HENRY. Let me be the voice of reason here. Paisley wants to fight for your honor.

Paisley: I do. I really do. Please let me do this.

Henry: Oh, all right. I know trying to get you to stop is like trying to catch the ocean in a mayonnaise jar.

Lizzie: You have such a way with words, Henry.

Henry: Thank you, Lizzie.

Paisley: And really, what could go wrong?

Henry: The last words of any fool before something goes horribly wrong.

Paisley: Oh, come on, Henry. Live a little.

Henry: Maybe you should seek counseling.

Madison: Maybe you should seek blood vengeance.

Paisley: I don't want to do anything physically to him, I swear. I just want to make him kind of miserable in small ways. Things that will poke at him for a day or two.

Lizzie: Or a week or two. I don't think lengthening the time frame of misery is too much to ask. Given what he put Henry through for years during middle school.

Henry: He was an asshole. I will give you that. But please don't do anything extreme.

Paisley: I promise not to do anything extreme.

Henry: Excellent. Keep me in the loop. I have to go to class now, but I'll be monitoring this situation.

Paisley: Excellent. Let's get to work.

Lizzie: Where do you want to start?

Madison: Yeah. I'm ready to help in any way possible. I've been dreaming of revenge plots for a long time.

Paisley: Well, I wasn't lying. I don't want this to be big stuff. I don't want to hurt him. I just want to . . . nudge him. To make life a little harder for him.

Madison: You work together, right?

Paisley: Yes.

Madison: I mean, there's plenty of stuff you can do there. Little things. Change his schedule, shred stuff instead of filing it, make him look bad in front of your boss.

Lizzie: I do want to echo Henry in saying that you need to be careful not to get yourself fired while trying to sabotage him.

Paisley: Yeah, I wouldn't be happy about that. That would be the worst kind of revenge. But I think I know how to temper this so that it's only little things that he'll notice and rub him the wrong way.

Madison: Yeah, that's the way to go.

Paisley: Our boss already gave him a warning. She's got a "three strikes and you're out" rule. I don't want to jeopardize our jobs. I want to set up small booby traps.

Lizzie: Love it. Booby traps have little to no consequence but they can make you miserable for a little while. It's the perfect way to think about this.

Paisley: And Henry will see. This will make me feel better. And it'll make Carter Schmitt reconsider crossing anyone ever again.

Lizzie: Is he still an asshole? I definitely remember him from back then and he was such a little asshole.

Paisley: I guess not really. I don't really focus on him very much. He was nice to me when we were making out?

Madison: Well, of course he was. He was getting what he wanted. Men. They're all the same.

Paisley: I'm going to keep brainstorming. I'll get back to you if I come up with anything great.

Madison: Me too.

Lizzie: Me three. I have a shift at the potato stand today.

Paisley: Aw, the potato stand. Good times. I miss working with you at the potato stand.

Madison: And I miss eating all of the potatoes.

Lizzie: John mentioned that if you want to come back over winter break to just let him know. He's sure someone will quit between now and then.

Paisley: I'll keep that in mind. I suddenly really miss the smell of potatoes and arguing with people about why we don't serve anything else. I'm sorry you got left there holding the bag, Lizzie.

Lizzie: *Shrug.* That's what happens when you go to community college and you live at home your first year of school. You get to keep your high school job.

Madison: All right, ladies, I have class. But we'll continue this later.

Paisley: Have fuuuuuuun.

Lizzie: Fun with a side of vengeance.

-Paisley has named the conversation "Fun with a side of vengeance"-

Madison: Lol.

Lizzie: Lol.

Paisley: Totally.

-CARTER-

Carter: Hey, Thea.

Thea: Hey, Carter.

Carter: How are things?

Thea: Things are fine. Remember? I texted you this morning?

Carter: Yeah, I know.

Thea: How are things with you?

Carter: They're okay.

Thea: Listen, obviously I can't read your mind, but it feels like things aren't all right. And it feels like you're texting me for a reason.

Carter: Yeah. I don't know. Everything maybe isn't fine.

Thea: Who do you need me to beat up?

Carter: Everyone? Would you be able to beat up everyone?

Thea: Maybe. I've been taking a cardio kickboxing class. (And yoga. You should take a yoga class. That might help.) Who should be first?

Carter: Me. Probably. Also, Paisley, my calc professor, and my boss at the gym, but it's really all my fault.

Thea: Well, let's take this one step at a time. How have these people wronged you?

Carter: They haven't! That's the problem. In all of these situations, I'm in the wrong. I got off on the wrong foot and now I can't find my way back to the right foot.

Thea: You've got some stuff going on.

Carter: I do, Thea. I have some stuff going on. I did shitty on my first calc exam, Paisley is still not speaking to me, and I think she's trying to get me fired.

Thea: Carter! That's not good! You can't let that happen.

Carter: I'm not going to "let" it happen. I don't have any control over it.

Thea: What did she do?

Carter: It's convoluted and I'm not actually, technically sure she did anything, but suffice to say, I have a strike on my record at work. I just didn't know how to argue it when it's her word against mine. I'm going to be more vigilant from now on.

Thea: Okay. Good. So, let's think of something you can do that can really help.

Carter: Like . . . ?

Thea: Like what might make you feel better. Obviously, you have control over calc. You need to get help with it. Visit the tutoring center, go to office hours. Stuff like that.

Carter: Yes. I've been going to office hours, but I do need more help. I wish Paisley didn't hate me or I'd ask her to help. I noticed she got an A on the exam.

Thea: Yeah, and if wishes were horses, beggars would ride.

Carter: I don't know what that means so I'm ignoring you and moving on.

Thea: Sure, sure. It's a fairly common saying, Carter.

Carter: Whatever, Thea.

Thea: Also, Carter. I'm sure there's a counseling center on campus. Don't forget how much therapy can help.

Carter: I know, I know. I'll keep it in mind.

Thea: ANYWAY. As you already mentioned, you'll be more vigilant at work and I think you really need to continue ignoring Paisley.

Carter: Yeah.

Thea: Are you not ignoring Paisley?

Carter: I mean, mostly.

Thea: Oh, Carter. I thought we talked about this! If she doesn't like you, you can't change that.

Carter: I'm not trying to change it! We sit next to each other at work for hours at a time. It's impossible to completely ignore her.

Thea: All right, fine. I accept that.

Carter: I think I need to start staying at school over the weekend. I need to get my schoolwork under control and maybe find a social life.

Thea: That's fine.

Carter: But then I feel guilty. Like I'm ditching you and mom for college, and college is kind of terrible, so maybe I should just go home.

Thea: We're getting along fine without you.

Carter: But you do so much! Letting Mom move in with you while she was sick, helping her sell our house. I don't do enough.

Thea: You do plenty. I'll keep a running list of things that are too high for me to reach until you come home next. ☺

Carter: Ha. Ha. Very funny.

Thea: I mean, that's really all I need you for.

Carter: You're so nice to me, Thea. (THAT IS SARCASM IN CASE YOU COULDN'T TELL.)

Thea: I know. I'm really kind. I hope this helped.

Carter: It did. It really did.

Thea: Good. Now go out there and get them!

Carter: Get who?

Thea: I don't know; it seemed like the thing to say.

Carter: Thanks, Thea.

Thea: There is something I need to tell you about, just so you know.

Carter: What?

Thea: Well, Dad found out that Mom was sick and he's been . . . around. Helping.

Carter: Sure. I'm sure that'll last a long time. He's so reliable.

Thea: He's been pretty reliable lately.

Carter: Good for him.

Thea: That's all you have to say?

Carter: As long as I don't have to see him, I don't care. I'm feeling better about my decision not to come home so much already.

Thea: Wow, Carter, such a great attitude.

Carter: You're the one who sprang this on me. I have to go do homework. Talk to you later.

-PAISLEY-

Henry: Can we talk?

Paisley: Of course.

Henry: I mean, do you have time to talk right now?

Paisley: Like on the phone?

Henry: Hell no. I just didn't want to interrupt you if you were busy.

Paisley: Listen, if this is about before, I'm really sorry if I wasn't paying enough attention to what you were saying, and if you're serious about it, I won't do anything to Carter. I got caught up in the moment. And the idea of giving him a zillion paper cuts like Lizzie suggested.

Henry: No, no, it's not that. Though I appreciate you saying it. I know you're going to do what you want to do. I really don't want you to get in trouble in the process. I'm not going to lie, though, I do feel a little, tiny bit of glee at the thought of you making him a teeny, tiny bit miserable.

Paisley: HA, I KNEW IT! I AM VINDICATED! Ahem. I mean. Yeah, cool. So what's up? Are you okay?

Henry: I need you to promise not to laugh at me. Or tease me about this. Or tell anyone else about it.

Paisley: Of course. Sure. I promise.

Henry: I have this huge crush on my TA.

Paisley: Is . . . is that all? Is your TA a man?

Henry: No, no. She's a girl. A woman. She's a JUNIOR.

Paisley: Nice, nice. Good for you! It's fun to have crushes.

Henry: But I'm, like, in love with her. I've never felt this way about anyone. Ever.

Paisley: Okay. That's tough when you feel that way.

Henry: And I think she came on to me?

Paisley: WOO-HOO!

Henry: But that's completely unethical! It would be morally repugnant for me to allow anything to happen between us!

Paisley: It would be morally repugnant if you exchanged grades for sexual favors, but a little flirting never hurt anyone. How did she come on to you?

Henry: She saw me in the campus center today and she sat with me.

Paisley: That's cool. She likes being around you.

Henry: But she said we should do it again sometime!

Paisley: Eat together again sometime?

Henry: YES.

Paisley: I'm not sure that qualifies as coming on to you. That seems more like, if you're there at the same time again, you should eat together again because she enjoys your company.

Henry: You think that's it?

Paisley: That's as far as I would read into it for now.

Henry: Oh good. I literally just sighed with relief. I feel so much better.

Paisley: Good. But you better let me know if anything else happens. Then I can interpret the interaction for you.

Henry: Yeah, cool. Thanks, Paisley. I really needed that.

Paisley: Anytime.

Henry: Good luck with your vengeance plot.

Paisley: Thank you, sir.

CHAPTER NINE

-CARTER-

"Party at my brother's house tonight," Ray says, bouncing into our room and dropping his backpack on the floor next to his bed. He has a brown grocery bag with him and carefully unloads everything into our mini-fridge.

I am, as usual, hunched over my desk doing homework, and now I have the added bonus of trying not to think about my dad. Life is grand.

"There's no way—" I start to say.

"Yes. There is a way," Ray interrupts. "You could just come."

Then I realize. I could go to the party. I'm not going home this weekend. I could get my homework done on Sunday night, rather than trying to rush through it on the train.

I slam my calc book closed.

"I had no idea you were so susceptible to peer pressure."

I laugh. "Well, I don't feel like going home this weekend. My mom and sister can get along without me. It's time to have some fun."

"Yes!" Ray says, fist pumping.

"So, is it a big party?" I ask, getting up from my desk and grabbing a drink from the fridge.

"Pretty big."

"Can you be a buffer between me and Paisley? I really don't want to see her."

"Dude. Of course. Also, nobody should ever keep you from having fun. Especially not Paisley. You have way more claim over this party than Paisley does."

"I'm not entirely sure that's true, but okay."

Ray rifles through his backpack and pulls out a small bottle of Jack Daniel's. "Luis gave this to me. You want some?"

"Maybe we should have dinner first?"

"You're, like, super smart. But pregame later, right?"

"Definitely."

-PAISLEY-

I have officially been called upon to be Stef's wingwoman. She's got a big old crush on one of the other girls on the swim team, and she needs backup at the party tonight. Pretty much the whole team will be there, apparently, because it's going to be one last hurrah before they start training in earnest for the upcoming season.

I can't believe I just used the phrase *one last hurrah*.

The only thing is, as soon as we get to the party, the girl Stef has a crush on, Melissa, invites her to play beer pong because her usual beer pong partner ditched her. So Stef is happily ensconced in a game, and I'm over here in the corner, much like I was the first weekend of school.

Ugh. That first party. I try not to think about that too much. Particularly now that Carter hates me as much as I hate him.

I could probably use a palate cleanser from that night. Someone to make me forget about my first kiss by giving me a second kiss. Maybe even a better kiss. A new pair of lips to focus on.

Especially since even after all this time, I sometimes have to stop myself from saying something to Carter along the lines of, "Let's go find a Ferris wheel and make out for a while." But I like to hope it's not about him so much as it about kissing and whatnot. At least I hope.

I scan the room. There are plenty of good-looking dudes in here, and I always have Stef to back me up. We did manage to come up with a signal in case one or the other is in need. A quick, casual pull on our right earlobe means, "PLEASE HELP ME NOW."

There's a guy pumping beer that I've had my eye on for a while. He's tall, even taller than Carter, more like a mountain than a tree. There's no one else near the keg so this seems like my best moment.

I wander over.

"Hey," I say.

"Hey," he says, grinning. "Are you on the team?"

"Nah, I'm Stef's roommate. Paisley." I hitch my thumb in her direction.

"Oh right, yeah. Gomez. She's a cool girl."

I want to correct him to say she's a cool woman, but we're just getting started. I can't hope that everyone is a perfect feminist right from the start. I can always mold him.

"Yeah, she is. We get along pretty well," I say, pumping up the keg and pouring myself a half of a Solo cup of beer. I still think the stuff tastes like ass, but it feels wrong not to at least have something in my hands.

"I'm Tommy."

We shake hands. Someone else comes up to the keg so we move out of the way.

"How come I haven't seen you around here before?" he asks.

"Do you live here?" I ask.

"Nah, I know Luis from the team."

"Yeah, we don't come to a ton of parties, I guess. But this isn't my first and it's probably not my last."

"I was watching you over in the corner, and I thought you were way too cute to be alone," he says, moving a little closer to me.

I clam up a little. Maybe this isn't what I want.

"You remind me so much of my little sister," he adds. I don't know what to say to that. But then the whole situation changes.

A girl wiggles up next to Tommy. "Hey, babe," he says to her. "Doesn't this girl remind you of my little sister?"

"Oh wow!" she says. "Totally."

She introduces herself as Tommy's girlfriend, Zoe. I'm about to walk away when she says, "I love your T-shirt!"

"Thanks," I say looking down at it. It's a cream-colored T-shirt that says A CUTE MESS. It's not my usual work. I had taken my time on this one, making the lettering extra neat and adding a floral design inside each individual letter. It was supposed to be for Lizzie, for her birthday, but after I washed it, I realized it had shrunk. I decided to make her a new one and keep this one for myself.

"Where did you get it?" Zoe asks.

"Um, well, I made it."

"OMG. Could you make me one? I'd pay like twenty bucks for a shirt that cute."

"Sure," I say, not mentioning that I bought the T-shirt at Walmart for six dollars. "Do you want to give me your email or number or something so I can contact you when it's done?"

We exchange information and then I have the most brilliant idea. I need to find Stef and tell her immediately.

-CARTER-

Ray and I walk into the party already kind of drunk. I immediately see Paisley on the other side of the room talking to some guy. He's enormous. Like twice my size. She seems into him, smiling at whatever he's saying to her.

Pisses me off. Between her and my dad and my strike at work and my shitty calc grade, I feel like I could explode.

I walk over to the keg and Luis is there.

"Hey, man," he says when he sees me and immediately starts pouring me a drink.

"Hey."

"I'm glad you came. Ray said he wasn't sure you would," he tells me, handing me the cup.

I shrug, but my anger is still barely simmering. I'm not sure what I find so annoying about Luis's statement, maybe that Ray has said anything about me, knowing that he probably said lots of other stuff. I try to push it aside.

I used to have a lot of anger issues, and it seems like they've all decided to come back right this second. I try to think of a coping mechanism, something that might help me not flip out in the middle of this basement. Or maybe it's just that liquor makes me angry. Maybe beer, as gross as it is, will chill me out.

"What did Ray say?" I ask through gritted teeth. It's like the angry monster has awoken inside of me. I was fine for so long and now everything makes me want to Hulk out.

"That you've been busy and your mom is sick. But I'm glad you could make it tonight. Everyone needs to blow off steam sometimes."

I take a long sip of beer and realize I lost Paisley in the crowd somewhere. At least that's a relief. "Yeah, you're right."

"I hope you don't mind that he told me," Luis says. "Is she okay? How's it going?"

"She's okay. I don't mean to bring you down during a party, but mostly she's fine. She had surgery. They got all the cancer." I don't add anything about my dad showing up out of the blue, mostly because I know that will make me angrier. Silently stewing about it is a better option.

Ray comes up to us then, slinging his arm around my neck. He has a bottle of beer from somewhere and I'm annoyed he didn't offer me one. Not that I think beer from a keg tastes any different than beer from a bottle. They all taste like cold piss to me.

"You in for beer pong?" Ray asks. "I signed us up, but if you're not feeling it, I'm sure I could convince Luis to play with me."

"I'm in," I say.

"Awesome," Ray says. "We're next. There are perks to being the little brother of the guy throwing the party."

-PAISLEY-

Tommy and Zoe move away onto the dance floor and I'm left once more entertaining myself. I gaze around the room looking for Stef but don't see her. I check all the usual spots and then I find her standing outside the bathroom.

"I had the most amazing idea," I say. It takes me a second to realize how sad she looks. "Hey, are you okay?"

She looks up at me. "She's dating someone. I had no idea she was unavailable."

"Aw, sweetie," I say, pulling Stef in for a hug.

"I just didn't expect this. Why didn't I expect this?"

"These things happen," I say, rubbing her arms.

"So, what's your big idea?"

"Oh, that seems silly now. You don't have to worry about me."

"No really. Tell me."

"I'm going to sell my T-shirts online."

Her eyes go wide. "That is a good idea. You get so many compliments on them. And I could wear one to all of my classes, like a walking billboard."

As we emerge out into the basement from the labyrinth of hallways that lead to the bathroom, it's only then that I notice Carter is here. Of course he is. I don't know how I didn't notice him earlier.

He's on a beer pong team with Ray versus Tommy and a guy I don't recognize.

Stef and I grab drinks and decide to dance for a while, to shake off her negative feelings and so she can show Melissa what she's missing.

"I think Carter is fighting for your honor," Stef whisper-yells, nodding in the direction of the beer pong table.

"What do you mean?"

"He probably saw you talking to Tommy earlier, got jealous, and now wants to show him who's boss."

I scoff.

"I'm serious," Stef says, dancing us a little closer. "Listen to how he's taunting Tommy."

It's true. Carter is showing his nasty streak. The one I know a little too well from middle school. Every time he gets the ball into a cup, he acts surprised and rubs it in Tommy's face.

I shrug. "It's his problem if he wants to be an asshole."

But I find myself keeping an eye on Carter from every angle of the dance floor. There's something about him tonight, like any little bit of pressure could make him blow. Like a dormant volcano.

As I have this thought, Ray and Carter win. They

high-five, but something is wrong. Tommy looks unhappy, of course. Carter's all smiles as the guy marches over to him.

I can't hear what's being said, but I have a bad feeling about it.

-CARTER-

On top of my rage issues, there's a good chance that I'm a sore winner.

This big guy is coming for me. I might as well let him.

I didn't expect to play against the guy who was hitting on Paisley before. I didn't expect to find myself taunting him the whole time. And I definitely wasn't prepared to win. Must be beginner's luck.

"You think you're so smart," he says to me, coming around the table.

"Good game," I say with a mean grin. Ray has walked over to the keg to fill the pitcher for the next round, so I'm on my own over here.

He just shakes his head. I'm drunk, but he's way drunker. I mean, that's sort of the point of beer pong, and losing beer pong is never going to help you sober up.

"You're a tiny asshole and I'm this close to smacking you down," he says. "You think you're so funny. Well, I've got news for you."

Before he can tell me his news, I catch sight of Paisley on the dance floor. I wind up and punch him in the face. It feels really good, at least until I realize that it also feels like my hand is broken. I shake it out, and as I turn to go, he punches me twice, once in the gut and once in the face.

And I'm going down.

-PAISLEY-

"Oh my god," Stef says. "What is Carter thinking?"

"He's not thinking. He's an asshole."

"Go help him," she says, pushing me in that direction.

"How?" I ask. "And also why?"

Stef gives me a look that I take as "you know why," so I slide between the people crowding around to step in between them.

"I see you're making friends, Carter," I say.

He looks up at me and shakes his head.

"Hey, it's you," Tommy says, obviously much drunker than he was earlier. "My little sister."

"Why'd you hit this guy here?"

"He hit me first."

"Look at him," I say. "He's tiny. Puny. A big guy like you? You shouldn't even be able to feel it if he hits you."

Luis comes up then and tells Tommy to go outside and cool off.

Tommy yells a few empty threats before taking off up the back stairs and out the door. I can't help feeling relieved.

Luis helps Carter stand.

"Well, that sucks," Carter says, his eye already swelling.

"What the hell just happened?" Ray asks, joining us in

the middle of the crowd. "I walk away for a second. You got a bad temper, dude."

Carter nods and holds his hand over his eye, like that's going to help.

"Come on," I say to him. I feel the need to take charge of this situation. Maybe I have Florence Nightingale syndrome, but I can't stand the idea that Carter is just going to get more and more drunk tonight, and probably pick more fights and wind up in a coma.

"Come on where?"

"Come on and we'll walk back to the dorm. We'll stop at the convenience store on the way for a bag of frozen peas."

He eyes me wearily.

"Come. On," I repeat. Then I turn to Ray. "I'm taking Carter home."

"That's probably a good idea. I'll come too."

I weave over to Stef to tell her we're leaving, but she decides to join us on our walk home.

"There's no reason to stay," she says, glancing back over at Melissa.

The four of us leave out the front door since Tommy is still out in the backyard. It seems like a good idea to avoid that situation entirely.

Tonight, as opposed to the first night, Carter walks several feet ahead of us, along with Ray, while Stef and I chat.

We stop at the convenience store along the way, where I buy Carter a bag of peas to use as an ice pack, and he and Ray both insist on getting slushies. As if I'm made of money.

I could probably go through his wallet and pull out some cash, but that seems wrong to me.

When we get to the building, he doesn't even thank me for saving him or for the treats he got at the store. He just grunts a goodbye and heads to his room. Ray, on the other hand, insists on a group hug, before showing us how blue his tongue is.

"Night, Paisley, night, Stef," he says, weaving lazily down the hallway behind Carter.

"This was a really weird night," Stef says.

"The weirdest," I agree.

"Let's go watch rom-coms and forget everything."

"You're a very smart lady."

"Why didn't we get slushies?" she asks in the elevator. "We deserved slushies too."

"We were so busy mom-ing them, we didn't take into consideration our own needs."

"So mom of us," she says. "Let's go raid the vending machines before the rom-com marathon."

"Now that's a good idea."

CHAPTER TEN

-CARTER-

I'm so hungover Saturday morning I almost forget that I have work at noon. It's not a normal shift for me. It's not a normal shift for anyone. But they need extra people today for some kind of prospective student event. Hopefully I can sit at the desk and check IDs without having to deal with Paisley.

No such luck, though. Guess who's standing at the desk when I walk in.

"Well, if it isn't Robinson Hall's very own Floyd Mayweather," she says with a shit-eating grin, as if being able to name one boxer makes her some kind of comedian.

I ignore her and head into the back office to stow my stuff. When I get to the desk, she's straightening up.

"Are you here all day?" I ask, my voice barely working. I take a sip of water followed by a long chug of coffee that I just grabbed from the back. Thank god I put so much milk in, so it's already cooled off.

"I'm off in . . ." She pauses to look at the clock. "Thirty seconds. You're on your own today. Luckily, it's been quiet. Everyone else is out at the event," she says, gesturing toward the back of the building.

"Fine."

"Somebody's in a great mood today."

I look over at her, trying to figure out what to say. I rub my temples, wincing when it pulls at the bruise around my eye.

"Are you okay?" she asks.

"What do you care?" I snap.

She blinks at me.

"You've made it abundantly clear on multiple occasions that you don't give a shit about me. So I'm not interested in your pity now."

"Okeydokey," she says without looking at me.

"That's all you're going to say?" I ask.

"What else do you want from me?"

-PAISLEY-

How dare he? Did I not step in between him and a behemoth of a man last night? Did I not walk him home? Did I not spend three dollars on overpriced peas so he could ice his face? Not to mention the two dollars on slushies. And now he's giving me attitude? How dare he?

And yet, he dares.

On my way back to my room, I take the long hallway to the stairs instead of the elevator up to the sixth floor.

This path leads me past Carter's room, which just so happens to be open and empty.

I need to use this opportunity.

I should take something of his.

I do a quick scan. One side of the room has a bunch of pictures stuck to the wall of people who look a lot like Ray. In fact, Ray is in quite a few of them. There's also the fact that he has a Brazilian flag stuck to his headboard.

I turn to the other bed. It's honestly a little sad-looking. Blue comforter, white sheets, no decor to speak of, minus Hula the unicorn sitting forlornly in one corner. I almost grab her.

But then the hum of the standard-issue mini-fridge clicks to a different frequency as if it's telling me to look inside.

There's not much in there. A slice of cake, a couple cans of soda, a Tupperware container of something, and of course, in the freezer, the bag of peas. I know Carter goes home a lot, and I would bet everything in my bank account (which isn't much) that this is all his food. Especially since I know the peas are his.

I pull everything out of the fridge and make a slit in the bag of peas. I take a handful out and shape them into a smiley face in the freezer. It's like my calling card. I'm sure Carter will be able to figure out it was me. But who cares?

I flee the scene of the crime, holding the stolen objects close as I run up the stairs. By the time I hit the sixth floor, I'm out of breath and almost start dropping things. I make it to my room and shove it all in our fridge, which is equally empty.

Also, the most important question of all: What am I doing? Why did I think stealing everything out of his mini-fridge was a good idea? I almost turn around and bring it all back, even if that means running into someone, but I can't quite bring myself to do it. I want to force him to come upstairs. I want him to come talk to me. I want to see him get angry. I want something to point to, to know that he's not any different. I hate admitting that, even to myself. But it's the truth.

-CARTER-

When I return from the worst work shift of my life, all I really want to do is lay down and take a nap. But first, I decide to shower.

Standing under the water, I ruminate over the worst work shift of my life. It included fun things like stampedes of people on guided tours, babies crying, children puking (okay, just one puker, but it seemed like more), and a super pissy boss. On top of my hangover and the pounding ache surrounding my black eye, it was hell.

But now I'm here. My bed is close. I was even smart enough to pick up a sandwich on the way home so I won't have to go back out to the dining hall anytime soon.

I eat the sandwich at my desk and scroll around the internet.

I wonder for a moment where Ray is.

I look over at his side of the room as I tear off my T-shirt and sit down on my bed. Hopefully he's not coming home anytime soon. I don't want anything to disturb my slumber.

Then it's finally time for the nap to end all naps. I pull the blinds down, queue up the perfect sleepy-time playlist, and pop in my earbuds. I adjust my pillow and fall asleep. Fast.

Which is why my anger ignites when I'm awakened what feels like seconds later by Ray banging around the room.

"What the hell, man?" he asks, but his voice is muffled. I realize that I still have my earbuds in even though my playlist has stopped. I grab my earbuds out and sit up.

"Huh?" I ask.

"Where is everything in the fridge? I had a bunch of leftovers in there from yesterday. Luis and I went home in the afternoon. It's all gone. Even the soda I put in there."

I stumble out of bed and look into the mini-fridge.

"That's so weird," I say, my anger changing to confusion.

"Where the hell did it go?" Ray is obviously pissed off. "It was leftovers from my sister's birthday dinner. Like birthday cake and everything."

I open the little door to the freezer and there's a smiley face made out of peas.

"I know what happened," I say

-PAISLEY-

I know it's Carter as soon as I hear the fist hammering at my door. I slide the chain and open the door as wide as it'll go. I've spent the morning working on T-shirts. I need to get out and buy more supplies, but first I have to sell off a couple, so I have money for said supplies. I figure I'll put what I have up online ASAP and send the link to Zoe. Maybe with a kindly worded email about sharing it with her friends.

"Yes, sir, how may I help you?" I ask in my most innocent voice.

His face is all red, and I am fully prepared to bear the brunt of his wrath.

"You stole my roommate's food."

"Hmm?" I ask, as if I couldn't hear.

"You stole Ray's food. They were leftovers from his mom. It's fine if you want to get back at me. But you don't have to bring Ray into it."

"I just assumed it was yours," I say, still keeping the door open only a few inches.

"Well, it wasn't."

"It's just a harmless little prank. I'm sure Ray will understand."

He puts his hand on his hip. "Yes. Totally harmless. Just enough to piss off Ray when we finally started getting along. So he'll blame me and we'll start fighting again. No big deal to you, though. Now please give me back his food. I don't think that's too much to ask."

I close the door to slide off the chain and let Carter in with a sigh. This is not the outcome I was looking for.

"You don't have anything to say?" he asks.

I go over to my mini-fridge without a word and hand him the food and sodas. I go to place the peas on top.

"Nah, I don't want the peas. You keep them. You bought them."

Ugh. I don't say it, but I think it.

"It's just that easy?" he asks.

I shrug.

"What was the point, Paisley?"

I don't have an answer. I finger the hem of the T-shirt I was screen printing on my desk.

DON'T GET MAD, GET EVEN, it says.

"What are you so mad about?" he asks, reading the shirt.

"Everything," I say.

"So, seriously, you don't have a reason for stealing this stuff?"

"I walked past your room earlier, your door was open, and no one was in there. That's about as far as the logic goes."

"But you knew I wasn't even home!"

I shrug for what feels like the millionth time.

"I don't know what the point of your game is. Do *you* know what the point of your game is?"

For a split second, I feel genuinely bad. I think maybe it's time for a truce, or at least a cease-fire.

"Somebody's gotta keep you on your toes, Carter. I don't want you getting soft on me. What if another guy slugs you in the face?"

"So, you giving me a hard time around every turn is because you don't want me getting soft?"

"Exactly."

"It's for my own good."

"You got it now."

"Doesn't screen printing cost a lot of money? How do

you always have the energy to make new T-shirts?" he asks, looking around the room, changing the subject.

"Oh, I don't screen print everything. Only the special stuff. Most of my T-shirts are iron-ons. Not like you care, but I'm going to start selling them online."

"That sounds"—he pauses and shakes his head— "completely pointless."

"Thanks."

"I'm just saying. It sounds like a lot of work for very little return. Senseless, futile even."

"Well, who asked you?"

He shrugs. "Nobody. But it seemed worth commenting on. Good luck with your future endeavors."

"Thanks so much," I say, folding my arms.

He turns on his heel and leaves.

-CARTER-

When I get back to our room, Ray is doing something on his laptop.

I show him the armful of stuff I retrieved. "So, Paisley stole all of this from our fridge."

"She did what now?" Ray spits out, laughing so hard he has to hold his stomach.

"Yeah, she said the door was open and no one was here so she stole it."

"Man, that's hilarious. I must have been down the hall for like three minutes, and that's when she came in. Sorry if I sounded pissed at you. It's actually kind of my fault."

"No worries. Who would have guessed she'd do something like that? Or that anyone would do something like that."

"She is really something else." He puts his leftovers in the microwave. "You want some?"

"Yeah, sure," I say. "Thanks."

"So what are you going to do?"

"Nothing?"

"I think you need to get even."

"See, but I feel like that's what she's been doing. She's been trying to get even with me for how she perceives that I wronged her in the past."

"Well, you did wrong her in the past. But now she stole my food and I want you to get back at her."

"Yeah?"

"Did you say she also pulled some shit at work?"

"Yeah. She got me in trouble." I pause for a second. "I think she pulled a screw out of my chair so I fell over."

"See? She's gotten back at you again and again. It's time to stoop to her level."

"What are you thinking?"

-PAISLEY-

Why can't things just be easy and normal?

Why do I spend so much time lately asking myself questions that don't have answers? Why did Carter have to ask me so many questions that don't have answers?

I spend the rest of the evening hanging out with Stef

and having a *Bring It On* movie marathon. I'm not ashamed that I like all of them. I also have a lot of T-shirts to make. I created an online shop this afternoon and sent the link to Zoe, who promptly sent it to a bunch of her friends, and now I'm almost drowning in orders. That'll show Carter. How dare he try to dampen my entrepreneurial spirit. I will put a T-shirt on every single person who goes to this school. Minus Carter. He can be left out.

On Sunday, I have the distinct urge to go out looking for Carter, so instead I put that energy into checking on Henry.

I call him, just for the fun of it.

"Why are you calling me?" he asks in lieu of hello.

"I'm calling to check on you. You seemed a little stressed out last time I talked to you."

"Give me a second," he says. "I'm studying in my room, but I don't want anyone to hear me talk about this."

I hear the distinct sound of a door closing and then some rustling.

"What are you doing?"

"I'm hiding in my closet. I figure the sound of my voice will be muffled in here."

"And you said I was being dramatic."

"So, what's up, Paisley?"

"Nothing. I'm calling to find out what's up with you, remember?"

"Ugh."

"*Ugh* is not an answer, Henry. Tell me about this girl."

He sighs. "She's a woman. She's twenty. She's my Calc

for Engineers TA. She is gorgeous. She's really nice to me. She's even Korean so my parents will love her."

"Does she have a name?"

"Jana."

"Nice. I like it. So what's the problem?"

"It is ethically promiscuous."

"I don't think it is."

"What if she likes me back?"

"Would that be . . . bad? I'm confused by your tone."

"It would be terrible, Paisley!"

"But you have the control here. You don't have to do anything if you're this worried about her liking you back. You can avoid the subject."

"What if she asks me out first?"

"Wait, has she officially asked you?"

"After class the other day, she mentioned how we had lunch together. And that we should do that again. And she was like, 'Or even dinner. Or coffee. Or something.'"

I stifle a laugh because I don't want Henry to think I'm laughing at him. But this is amazing! This woman might actually like him. Not that Henry is unlikable. Lots of girls liked Henry in high school. But he has this person on such a high pedestal he might not even notice.

"What did you say?" I ask.

"I tripped over a chair and the subject was dropped."

This time I don't stifle my laugh. "Ah, Henry. That sounds about right. At least you didn't go into a fugue state."

"Small blessings." I can imagine the rueful expression on his face.

"Well, I'm here to talk about this whenever you need to, but I'm pretty sure you have it under control."

"Do I?"

"Yes. You totally do. You don't have to do or say anything you don't want to."

"Right. You're right. I know you're right."

"But?"

"But what if I want to?"

"You want to be ethically promiscuous?"

"Maybe?"

"Well, just keep it in your pants until the end of the semester and then make sure that you don't take her section next time, if she's still TAing. If she hasn't been let go for being ethically promiscuous."

He laughs this time, and I can sense that he's feeling better.

Which in turn makes me feel better.

Maybe everything is going to be fine.

CHAPTER ELEVEN

-CARTER-

Everything is clearly the worst. Minus the fact that Ray and I are finally on good terms.

It's Monday morning, and Paisley is wearing her DON'T GET MAD, GET EVEN shirt to class.

When she comes over to the desk, I show her the memo that had been posted.

"Have you seen this?"

It's an employee memo about no public displays of affection or sexual congress of any kind in the fitness center by students, faculty, guests, and employees of the fitness center.

"What is it?" she asks.

"We have to uphold a standard of behavior in the fitness center. 'If you are caught engaging in any type of sexual congress while on the clock, you will be fired,'" I read out loud.

"Certainly doesn't have anything to do with us," she says, her voice snippy.

"I thought maybe you'd heard something."

"What, like gossip? You want to gossip with me, Carter?" she asks. But it's obviously rhetorical because she doesn't even wait for me to respond before opening her calc book and getting right into her homework.

I just don't get her. And I'm tired of trying.

Our shift seems to drag on and on. And somehow, the classes we have together are even worse.

We've never sat next to each other in any of our classes, so it doesn't really change anything, but for some reason today, her very presence in each room feels like a splinter someplace uncomfortable. Like under my fingernail or in my eye. Not a normal splinter.

We get our papers back in history. A paper we've been working on for weeks. We had to hand in a proposal, an outline, and a first draft. I thought I was doing pretty well on it, even though all the lead-up assignments were only graded pass/fail.

Turns out for once I was right. There's a big red A on it. I can't help glancing over to where Paisley is sitting a few rows up from me. Even from here I can clearly see a C on her paper. I smile down at my desk.

Back in our room later that afternoon, Ray is playing a drum solo on his desk with a couple of pencils. I'm about to throw something at him.

"So," he says, keeping the beat on his notebook. "I've been brainstorming ways to get back at Paisley."

"Oh yeah? Come up with anything?"

Ray scratches his head. "She lives up on the sixth floor?"

"Yeah, are you thinking of taking something?"

"Maybe instead of taking something, we leave something?"

"Like what?"

"I don't know. Like a condom full of conditioner."

I laugh, but that makes me uncomfortable. I'm torn, though, because this is the most fun that Ray and I have ever had. At least since the first weekend of school.

He shakes his head. "Nah, that wouldn't be cool. Funny but not cool. But something like that, you know? Something kind of annoying, maybe a little bit gross."

I start googling.

He must think I'm going back to my work because then he says, "Yeah, we don't have to do it now. We should probably get back to work anyway."

"What?" I ask. "No. I'm looking up pranks! I'm not very good at that stuff, but I like the idea. We could come up with something at least. Just some minor payback."

Over the next couple of days, ideas for pranking Paisley become something that we bond over.

Ray will send me a text or mention something to me in our room. We discuss a wide variety of typical college pranks to play on her, water glasses all over her room or nailing her furniture to the ceiling.

There's something cathartic about even discussing the idea. Most of them I reject because I don't want to piss off Stef. She doesn't deserve to be pulled into Paisley's and my shenanigans. Also, she seems like the kind of person who would not appreciate getting pranked, no matter how innocent it is.

We need to find the right blend of funny and harmless.

It's thanks to all this research that I'm ready when the opportunity arises. She leaves her phone unattended at work. I've noticed she doesn't have a passcode on it. She's about to learn her lesson.

I make a couple of quick changes to her keyboard short-cuts. Anytime she tries to type "hey," "what," or "you," the phone will autocorrect that to "Carter Schmitt is the best."

I put her phone down just in the nick of time.

It's Monday, so we have three classes in a row and I can't wait for her to figure out what I did.

I see her check her phone a few times during our first class, and as we're walking out, she starts typing.

"What the hell," I hear her mutter. I turn around just in time to see her shake her phone up and down, as if that's going to help.

As she walks by me, face screwed up in concentration, I say, "Maybe next time you won't leave your phone un-attended."

"Thanks for this," she says, holding up her phone. "Now my mom thinks I'm in love with you."

I crack up so hard; I practically fall over there in the hallway.

"Oh man, it's even better that it was texts with your mom." I hold my hand up for a high five, and for a split sec-ond, I almost think she's going to do it.

Instead she turns on her heel and stalks off. Doesn't even look at me for the rest of the day. But I can't help grinning every time I think about it.

I feel lighter than I have in weeks.

-PAISLEY-

Stef and I are in the dining hall, selecting the perfect dinner, when her crush Melissa appears out of nowhere.

I can feel Stef tighten up beside me when she sees her.

I was in the midst of complaining about Carter's dumb shortcut prank, but this takes precedence. I still can't believe he thought I was going to high-five him over pranking me. Like I'm that stupid.

"We'll get through the line and then find somewhere far away from her to sit," I say quietly. I'm actively ignoring the fact that I got a C on my history paper, and getting involved in this small drama in Stef's life is a great distraction.

"Thanks," Stef says.

We find a table far in the back corner, out of sight from where the swim team usually sits, and therefore, hopefully out of sight from Melissa.

"I can't believe I didn't know she was dating someone. And it's a guy," Stef tells me. "Not that there's anything wrong with that. Like, she's bi, I'm a lesbian. That's fine. But it was so unexpected."

She takes a big bite of mashed potato, expression thoughtful.

She swallows and says, "That's definitely why I didn't realize she was in a relationship. I just thought she was flirty with everyone. Not that she was actually dating him."

I don't bother asking "Him who?" only because the swim team bench goes deep and I have trouble keeping up with the members. Stef doesn't mind. She made up the rule herself because it's really hard to keep explaining who people are. I know the important ones. The people she's friends with, the girl she has a crush on, and, of course, Luis of the epic parties and the brother of Carter's roommate.

This is good. I'm in a good place. Helping Henry with his girl trouble and now helping Stef with hers. I mentally pat myself on the back.

"Oh god," I say.

"What?" Stef asks.

"Do not look now," I say through mostly closed lips, trying to remember anything from the ventriloquism book I read when I was in third grade, "but Melissa is coming over here."

"No!" Stef yelps, just as Melissa steps next to our table.

"Hi," she says, all perky and bouncy curls.

"Hi," I say.

"Hey," Stef says. "Sorry about the yell. I thought I lost my wallet."

Melissa chuckles. "Do you kids mind if I sit with you?"

"So, how are the mashed potatoes?" Melissa asks when she's settled.

"Decent," Stef says. She stares at me and I make a confused face.

Melissa turns to me too. "Did I see you coming out of Professor Brightly's class today?"

"Yup," I say. Brightly is the professor who gave me a C on the paper I poured my blood, sweat, and tears into over the past three weeks.

"A word of advice," she says. "Make sure you take

copious notes. Brightly only tests on the notes. And she wants to see stuff in all your papers that she mentions in class. It's kind of like she wants Easter eggs in everything."

"Well that explains why I got a C on my paper. I take the worst notes," I say.

Melissa says she'll check if she has her notes from last year, but she's pretty sure she tossed them.

"That would be awesome," I say.

"So what were you talking about when I walked up? You looked like you were having a serious discussion," Melissa says. "I almost didn't want to interrupt."

"Um," Stef says.

"I was telling Stef about this dumb prank a guy at work played on me!" I say, nearly shouting.

"Oh, a prank war," Melissa says, nodding. Stef looks so relieved not to have to come up with a lie.

"I guess that's what this is," I say. "I just don't know how to play my next move."

"Well, if you ask me, you can never go wrong with a classic. Salt in his coffee or something like that. Doesn't hurt him but definitely pisses him off."

"Are you a prank expert?" Stef asks.

Melissa shakes her head. "I grew up with too many brothers and cousins and neighborhood boys who were always trying to make life miserable for each other. They left me out of it for the most part, but I learned a few tricks."

"You are just full of useful information," I tell Melissa. I can see why Stef is so into her.

The conversation moves on, but a few minutes later something clicks in my head. If Melissa doesn't have her notes from last year, I'm going to have to ask someone in my history class for notes. Someone besides Carter.

I'm going to have to make a friend.

That task seems daunting.

Maybe I'll just fail the class instead.

-CARTER-

You'd think I'd be smart enough not to leave my stuff lying around after what I did to Paisley's phone the other day, but you'd be wrong.

Which is why I'm honestly not shocked when I return from the bathroom to find that Paisley has put salt in my coffee.

"Hmmm," I say, rather than spitting it out.

She looks over at me and pushes a lock of hair behind her ear. I hate when she's cute.

"Good coffee?" she asks, a genuine look of glee on her face.

"Delicious. Must have gotten a new blend in the office," I say, taking a large gulp. It honest to god tastes like it was brewed with seawater, but I'm not going to let Paisley know I think so.

"That's so great. I'll have to try it later."

"You really will," I say, swigging the rest.

She starts to laugh.

I start to laugh.

"It was like a salt lick," I say, my eyes tearing up. "How much did you put there?"

"Way more than I meant to," she confesses.

I can't believe we're having a genuine moment over her putting salt in my coffee.

Which is why I'm still thinking about it later when Ray finds me in the quiet study room on our floor. Now that my grade in history is secure, I need to seriously buckle down and get my calc grade up.

I check the time on my phone as he walks through the door, and I have a missed call and a voice mail from an unfamiliar number. I'm pretty sure it's my dad. I have to stop myself from immediately deleting the voice mail and blocking the number.

Thea had warned me that he'd asked our mom for our numbers. But why would she actually give them to him? Why is my mom being nice to my dad when he screwed her over the way he did?

I flip my phone over onto the table and turn my attention to Ray who's standing there with barely contained glee on his face.

"I had an idea!" he says, way too loudly for the quiet study room.

Luckily, I'm the only person in here at the moment.

"I'm proud of you, Ray."

He rolls his eyes. "I had an idea of the getting-back-at-Paisley variety!"

"Oh, good," I say. "Because she salted the heck out of my coffee this morning. I'm glad to hear you're committed."

"Of course I'm committed. That woman stole a slice of my mom's coconut cake. She's just lucky it got back to me unharmed."

"So, what's the plan?" I ask, closing my calc book. I think revenge sounds like way more fun than calculus.

"Post-its," he says, showing me a picture on his phone. Someone had covered a bed, desk, and dresser in Post-its.

"I like it. Minus the fact that Post-its cost a lot of money and I have no idea how we would get into Paisley's room for that length of time to completely cover all of her belongings."

"Oh, right," he says, his face falling.

"But I like where your head is at," I tell him, not wanting to discourage him, especially now that I'm really in the mood to do something.

"Well, my other idea was hot sauce," he says.

"Hot sauce?"

"Yeah, I have some seriously hot Brazilian hot sauce— do you guys ever eat at work?" he asks, interrupting himself.

"Sometimes. She'll have a bagel or something but usually only on Saturday mornings, and we haven't been scheduled together on a Saturday morning in a while."

"Hmm. Well, I can give you a little bottle, and when you get the chance, you could sprinkle a little on her food. She'll be crying in no time."

"Another really good idea, but I want to do something now, you know? Like what could we do to her right this second? Not at some random time in the future when all the stars align and I can get some hot sauce onto her Saturday-morning bagel."

He taps his fingers on the table. "You're right. And whatever we do to her, I want to see it happen because she stole *my* food."

"Right, you're a part of this vendetta and you deserve to be there when it goes down."

"Maybe it's time we stop worrying about pissing Stef off in the process," he says.

"Yeah, I was kind of thinking the same thing."

"Did you have anything in mind?"

That's how Ray and I find ourselves outside Paisley's door at four in the morning, duct-taping her and Stef in.

"She's going to be so pissed off," I say, barely able to stop myself from giggling. We added a sign on the inside of the tape that says "Good morning, sunshine!" She's going to kill me. Stef is going to kill me.

But I'm not sure I care.

Ray is barely even awake, but he's doing a good job of cutting strips of tape while I stick them across the doorjamb.

He yawns as we step back to look at our work.

"Good job," he says, patting me on the back.

We shuffle back to the elevator to head down to our room.

"I can't believe no one saw us doing this," I say.

"I can't believe we're not going to have live footage of her trying to get out."

"We should have installed one of those cameras, like the ones they have on roller coasters."

"Does she have work this morning?" Ray asks.

"No."

"Do you?"

"Nope?"

"So maybe in a couple hours we should go back up there and wait and see what happens."

"Genius," I say.

We get back to the room, and I set my alarm for 8:00 a.m. I can't imagine anyone will need to get up any earlier than that.

But then Ray springs out of bed with a yelp.

"What? What is it?"

He shakes his head, his eyes holding a haunted look. "Stef has swim practice this morning at seven. She's going to be so pissed!"

"Hmm. And it's not even going to really affect Paisley."

"Well, it will because Stef will really be that pissed. It's going to take her a while to get out of there, and Paisley will have to deal."

"Yeah, good point."

Ray gets back into bed. "But I don't think we need to get up to watch that."

"Even better point," I say. I turn off the alarm on my phone and roll over, falling easily back to sleep.

CHAPTER TWELVE

-PAISLEY-

It's very early in the morning when I hear Stef cry out from somewhere near the door. I leap from my bed, grabbing for Debra the zebra because she's the nearest projectile, not because I continue to sleep with her.

Fine. I continue to sleep with Debra the zebra.

"What? What is it?" I ask, bleary-eyed. There's a weird kind of light coming from the doorway.

"What the heck?" I ask.

Stef still hasn't said a word, so I flick on the closest light. It looks like there's a cocoon crisscrossing our doorway.

Stef has her fingers knotted in her hair, just staring at it.

"I overslept," she says, her voice carefully metered. "And I need to be at the pool in the next seven minutes. But I can't leave our dorm room."

"I don't even understand."

She hands me a piece of paper. "Good morning, sunshine!" it says. "Have fun unraveling yourself!" Then there's a heart followed by the letters *C* and *R*.

"Looks like Carter and Ray had a bit of fun during the night."

Stef shrieks. I've never seen her look so stressed out. "What am I supposed to do about this?"

"It's fine. We'll get out of here. I'm sorry you're going to be late to swim practice, but it's not like I asked for this."

She rolls her eyes.

I grab for my scissors on the desk and start stabbing and cutting into the tape. There must be several layers.

"Are you going to help me or are you just going to stand there watching?" I ask Stef. "Because you'll get out of here sooner if you help."

She makes another sound of frustration, something between a grunt and a "harrumph," but puts down her toothbrush and face wash and grabs her scissors.

"I swear to god if they did any damage to the paint around our door and we get fined . . . ," she says as we work through the layers and layers of tape.

"If that happens, we'll explain it wasn't us, and Carter and Ray will have to pay," I say.

"Sure, that sounds good now. But they'll just deny it."

"Listen, that's the least of our worries right now, isn't it?"

"Whatever," she says. We finally make a hole big enough for her to fit through.

"Go," I say. "I'll finish this."

She looks like she might cry. "You know, it might be

time to call a truce with Carter or something. This is really shitty."

"Stef, this is not the time to talk about this," I say, prodding her in the side. "Go."

She nods and jumps over the paper. I see her make a quick stop at the bathroom to brush her teeth and I get back to work trying to free our doorway.

It takes almost a half hour and the entire time I'm seething. I've never been so angry in my life. Probably because it was one of my few days this week to sleep in. I begrudgingly admit to myself that this is a fair response to coffee salt and stealing Ray's food.

Though I'll never admit that to Carter.

I had this moment yesterday, when we were laughing about him drinking all that salty coffee, where it was like my body remembered how much I like him. How much I *liked* him. It's a hard truth to come to terms with that I still find him attractive and charming and all that other garbage. But the feelings are there.

I stand in the hallway when I'm done, surveying the area. There's not much damage to the paint around the door. Luckily. I'd be even more pissed if we were going to get fined for Carter's dumb prank. It might take a while to get all the sticky residue off, but that's better than lots of damage.

Carter should prepare for my revenge. It will be severe. Especially since he was so high-and-mighty about how my little food-stealing prank would affect his relationship with his roommate. Then those two fools go and do this.

I shake my head. I really need a good plan.

But first, I need a good T-shirt to wear to work tomorrow.

-CARTER-

When I get to work the next day at 6:01, Paisley is already inside, setting up for the morning. I was surprised that Paisley totally avoided me yesterday. It didn't exactly take much effort since we only have one class together, but still. I wanted to get her reaction to the tape prank, but she's playing it all pretty close to the vest.

As I pass through the office, I put on a pot of coffee, which I've gotten much better at making over the past few weeks, if I do say so myself. I make my usual rounds, turning on lights and making sure doors are unlocked. Paisley and I can do the morning setup on autopilot.

Then I head back out to the desk just in time for Paisley to unlock the doors and the first people of the day to wander in. I will never understand how or why some people look so awake at six thirty in the morning. What time do you have to go to bed to look that awake at six thirty in the morning?

Paisley's wearing a T-shirt that says "Good morning, sunshine," so she obviously has some kind of feelings about my prank. It's just weird that she's not verbalizing them.

I take my seat and a loud fart sound echoes through the front foyer, and I jump out of my chair. Everyone who was entering or leaving the gym pauses for a second, a few look annoyed but most smile and chuckle. One lady doubles over with laughter.

"A whoopee cushion?" I ask, holding it up.

Paisley smirks at me.

"That's the best you could do?"

"It's a classic for a reason," Paisley says. "And I'm sure there's more where that came from."

Her ominous warning leaves me tiptoeing around work for the rest of our shift and the next couple of days.

I need to be ready with some kind of mutually assured destruction. I just don't know what that looks like in this case.

A whoopee cushion isn't exactly that big of a deal, but there were plenty of people wandering through the fitness center at that moment and I'm sure I blushed beet red.

I feel an escalation coming on. I won't even use the hand sanitizer at the desk for fear that she's put something in it.

Maybe I should put something in the hand sanitizer at the desk.

I check the work schedule. We're on again together on Wednesday. I'll be ready.

-PAISLEY-

It's cold and dark tonight on the walk to the dining hall for dinner. I guess that makes sense; it is almost the end of October.

Stef shoves her hands deeper into the pockets of her fleece.

"So what's up with Carter these days?" she asks.

I laugh a little maniacally. "I have him right where I want him. He's so nervous, just waiting for me to plan out my revenge plans. I put a whoopee cushion on his chair this morning, and when he sat on it, he turned, like, so red."

"Oh yeah?" Stef asks, smirking a little.

"I've been trying to think of a way to get back at him and Ray together, but I haven't come up with anything."

"Paisley, you know I love you, right?"

"Sure, but that kind of sentence is never followed by anything good."

She rolls her eyes. "You say you hate Carter over and over again, but you obviously enjoy his attention. You're really enjoying this prank war, which seems to be like an excuse to, I don't know, think about him and talk about him and spend time with him."

I deflate a little. I was worried someone might notice that. I'm not surprised it was Stef. "Yes. I know."

"No argument?"

"I can sense my own hypocrisy on this topic, and I just don't have anything solid to debate with you."

"Wow. I feel like you're really growing as a person."

"Thanks."

"What's the next step then? Do you have a plan for a prank that doesn't involve Ray?"

"I've been thinking about something class related?"

She sucks in a breath through her teeth. "That might not be the best idea. You don't want to mess around with his grades or anything."

"I mess around with his job," I point out.

"Well, yeah, maybe you shouldn't be doing that either."

"Maybe."

"I feel like getting him fired or him getting in trouble in class wouldn't be very good for your own karma."

I nod. "It's like, I know you're right. But I don't want you to be right."

"I understand."

"What's up with Melissa?" I ask as we enter the dining hall.

"I got to hang out with her and her boyfriend at practice today. We were running drills and ended up all in the same group. PDA should be illegal during swim practice. Talk about ugh," Stef says.

"So nothing good for either of us then?" I say.

She shakes her head. "Seems that way."

We join the end of the snaking dinner line.

"We need to remember to come earlier," I say.

"For real," she agrees.

"At least it's pasta night."

"At least," Stef says.

"When's the next time you see Carter?" Stef asks as we find a table.

"Is today Tuesday?"

"Yes."

"Then tomorrow."

"Hmm. It'd be good to come up with something between now and then."

I nod. But I don't know what.

When I get to work the next morning, Carter is already there, setting everything up. Which is all well and good, seeing as how half the time I get there long before he does, but it's still a little disconcerting.

"Hey," I say, taking a seat at the desk.

"Hey," he says.

The morning goes pretty quietly. Around eight o'clock, Jordan comes in. "I just had to wash so much bird crap off my car."

She grabs for the hand sanitizer on the desk and pumps a ton of it into her palm, placing the bottle back on the desk and working it through her fingers.

Carter looks up and his face goes white. "No!" he shouts.

"What?" Jordan asks.

She looks at her hands.

They're bright blue.

"What the hell?" she asks, grabbing several tissues and trying to wipe off the coloring.

"I might have put food dye in the hand sanitizer. But it wasn't meant for you! It was meant for Paisley," he says sheepishly.

Jordan shakes her head. "You two have got to stop whatever is going on here. I can tell there have been a lot of games being played at this desk. I've turned a blind eye because it hadn't affected your work or anyone else. But now"—she pauses and holds up her hands—"now it's turned my hands blue, and I have a presentation to make today for a grant proposal and I look like a Smurf."

"Sorry, Jordan," we say in unison.

"Paisley, I hope you learn something from this. I can't exactly punish you for something Carter did, but you're on thin ice. And, Carter, come see me in my office."

-CARTER-

After work and class, I decided that what I really needed was a nap. Especially since my head was pounding. Probably from the fact that I got in trouble at work. Another strike on my record doesn't look great for me. I can't lose this job. I need the money.

I go down to the vending machine and get a Coke, knowing the sugar and caffeine can only help at this point. Especially since I have so much work to do. Except that I'm starving.

I pick up my phone to text Ray to ask him to bring me back a burger and fries from the student center, and I see a text from Thea.

> **Thea:** I'm taking Mom to the hospital. She can't keep anything down.

Suddenly I feel like I can't keep anything down. I almost want to spit out the sip of soda I just took. I swallow hard around the lump that grew in my throat while reading the text.

> **Carter:** I'm on my way.

> **Thea:** No, you're not.

Carter: Yes. I am. You can't stop me.

Thea doesn't respond to that, which only makes me want to get home even faster.

Carter: I gotta go home. My mom is in the hospital. It's an emergency.

Ray: I hope everything is all right. Let me know if you need anything.

I want to say something back to him, but I don't even know what that would be at the moment. My brain is whirling a mile a minute.

I throw whatever I can think of into my backpack before I head toward the train station off campus. I hop on the next train and sit for the long hour. I open my calc textbook and stare at the numbers. Nothing seems to be penetrating my brain, but it's better than thinking too much about my mom.

It's the kind of night where it's not raining but the air is so wet that I end up looking like a drowned rat by the time I get to the hospital.

My mom has been admitted for the night, and a nurse directs me where to go. Thea is in the room when I get there.

"I told you not to come," Thea says when she sees me.

"As long as Dad's not here, it's the only place I want to be."

Thea huffs out an exaggerated sigh. "We'll talk about that later," she says.

I walk over to Mom and kiss her cheek. "I'm fine," she says. "You shouldn't be here. You have more important things to do."

She's not wearing a wig or a scarf, and her hair has grown back in uneven peach-fuzz tufts.

I gesture toward it. "This is a good look for you."

"Oh, Carter," she says with an eye roll.

I feel so much better just being here. There's so much relief in seeing my mom, even if she is sitting up in a hospital bed attached to an IV.

"You really didn't have to come," Thea says. "I have it under control."

"I had to."

"You really didn't," my mom says. "But I'm glad you're here."

Suddenly everything that was wrong with this day, this week, this past month doesn't matter. Everything is okay if my mom is okay.

Thea settles into a chair, and I hop up in the bed next to my mom and it feels cozy. At least as cozy as things can feel in a generic hospital room. My mom rubs my arm like she would when I was little, and nothing feels like a big deal, not even my problems at work or my worries about my calc grade.

"It's good to see you, Carter," my mom says.

"You too, Mom," I say, resting my head on her shoulder.

All too soon the doctor comes in and shoos us out; visiting hours have long been over and my mom needs her rest.

Thea and I get in the car.

"Distract me," Thea says before I can ask any questions.

"What?"

"Distract me," she repeats. "We have a fifteen-minute drive home and I don't want to talk about Mom. I want to hear about your boring everyday life."

"Well, I got in trouble at work today." I relay the story and Thea *hmm*s and *ahh*s at all the right moments.

"So you're locked into a prank war with Paisley. I feel like she'll never let go of this grudge about you lying to her. Not if she's still holding a grudge from middle school. I don't think there's a good way out of this."

"Yeah, I just feel like I'm so close to . . . something. Like she doesn't hate me the way she used to, even with the pranks we're playing."

The streetlight spotlights Thea's face through the rain-soaked windshield. "I don't think it's worth it, Carter. I don't like being the voice of reason, but it just seems like she's getting you in trouble at work. She might not have boundaries. She might get you into lots of other trouble."

"I know. To hear you say it out loud really puts it into perspective."

"So you can be civil, but it's time to get past it."

"How do I end the prank war?" I ask.

"Well, ignore it. If she pranks you again, just don't engage."

"Don't engage," I repeat. "I can do that."

"Good."

We pull into the driveway.

"Any further thoughts before we go inside and I have a glass of bourbon and take a long hot bath?"

I shake my head. "Nah. But I really needed this."

She's about to open her door. "You didn't ask about Dad."

"There's nothing I want to know."

We walk into the house in silence and then part ways. I have a lot to think about.

CHAPTER THIRTEEN

-PAISLEY-

When Carter doesn't show up for class the next morning, I'm almost a little worried. He's always in class.

I don't have his number so I can't text him. If someone had asked me a week ago, I would have taken a smug pride in the fact that I didn't have Carter's number, but now I have regrets. I'd kind of like to check on him.

On the other hand, I assume we're not on speaking terms after the incident with Jordan yesterday. I know the hand sanitizer prank was a preemptive strike against me, and it feels a little wrong that he got in trouble and I didn't. On the other hand, he did dye Jordan's hands a bright shade of blue, something I had no part of, even if it was a battle in our prank war.

Maybe it's time for a cease-fire.

Or maybe I need to get back at him one last time and *then* call a cease-fire.

My problem is that a cease-fire, to me, has become synonymous with friendship. Like, I don't see it going any other way. Once we stop pranking each other, we're going to end up being friends. I know I could stop that by, you know, not being friends with him. But it's too hard. He's too nice. He's too good.

He's proven over and over again that he's not the same kid from middle school. And that the deception the first weekend of college was not indicative of his actual personality. It was a blip. A mistake.

I'm so glad that no one can read my mind. This is all rather embarrassing, considering how much I hated him not so long ago.

But there's still part of me that feels like I can't trust him.

That still feels like he owes me something.

My last class gets out early, so afterward, I decide to take a walk to the grocery store. I walk to the off-campus one, even though it's on the smaller side, but at least it's not as overpriced as the convenience stores on campus. A dollar for a banana? Please.

I'm wandering the aisles, debating what I want, versus what I need, versus what will fit in our mini-fridge, versus what I'm strong enough to carry back, versus ultimately what I can afford.

It's a balancing act for sure.

Part of this errand is because I'm avoiding T-shirt orders. Between Stef wearing them to class and Zoe telling her friends about them, I can't keep up. And I've already had several people contact me about holiday orders. Like what the heck, people, it's not even Halloween yet.

I'm considering texting Stef to see if she needs anything when I catch sight of something unexpected in the dairy aisle.

Carter has come in with two women; I assume one is his sister and the other, I know, is his mom.

But she's wearing a head scarf and looks kind of green tinged. She was our class mom back in elementary school, first or second grade. She made cupcakes and went on field trips with us. I remember I always liked her because she didn't just talk to Carter. She talked to all of us. And she would switch around who she sat next to on the bus.

She always had some game or song or idea to keep things interesting.

But now. She's pretty obviously sick. Like, cancer sick.

I scoot around the edge of the store, not wanting to call any attention to myself.

My phone buzzes in my pocket. I'm standing in the middle of the cereal idea, so I duck behind a display of Cheerios. I don't need to be out in plain sight.

It's Henry.

Henry: I'm texting you so that Jana doesn't notice me and try to talk to me.

Paisley: That sounds like a terrible plan. Though I do have to warn you that I'm currently grocery shopping and spying on Carter's family. Keep texting me even if I don't answer.

Henry: Carter's family?

Paisley: Yeah, they just came into this store and it looks like his mom is sick.

Henry: Sick how?

And then I feel a tap on my shoulder.

-CARTER-

My mom is released in the morning, and she insists on coming for the ride with Thea to bring me back to school.

"You should go home and rest," I say.

"*You* should go home and rest," she says.

I grin because I can't help myself. Everything feels so much better this morning.

"And this way we can make sure you have a good meal. Isn't there an off-campus place that everyone raves about?" she asks my sister.

Thea nods. "Are you really up for it?"

"My stomach is empty, and as long as I don't eat too much, I'll be fine. I'm sure they have something simple on their menu. Maybe a good soup."

When we get back to school, Thea drives us directly to the restaurant, which is good because I'm starving. We walk in and take our seats. I'm happy to see my mom eating pretty normally.

When we're done eating, Thea offers to bring me to the grocery store to pick up snacks or soda or whatever. And guess who's lurking the aisles?

Paisley.

I really didn't want her to know about my mom. Like, I can deal with Paisley in a million different ways and I can take all the hits she wants to give me, but this is private.

The prank war has been kind of fun and all, minus the part where I got in trouble at work, but I know for Paisley the emphasis is on the "war" part and I really don't need her trying to take advantage of me somehow because my mom is sick. And I just . . . didn't want her to know. I don't know how else to explain it. But I guess she'll know now.

I let my mom and my sister walk up to the front to pay, and I slip down one aisle and then another. I find Paisley hiding behind a stack of Cheerios. I tap her on the shoulder and she jumps.

"I know what you're doing," I say.

"Grocery shopping?" she says, as she stows her phone in her bag.

"Watching me. Stalking me like prey," I say. I do my best to make it sound like a joke, but I have this weird feeling like it might be true.

"Me?" she asks, pointing at herself, all innocence. "Little old me? Why would I be watching you? Why would I stalk you like prey?"

I cross my arms.

"Carter, I'm not going to play a prank on you here in the aisles of the Acme. This is a random bump-in. I was not prepared to prank you in any way, shape, or form."

"I almost want to ask you to dump out your bag. But I'll trust you. This time."

She grins. I can't help but grin back. Seeing her, it's like I can't help think about how good we could be together. But then I remember the talk I had with Thea last night.

I'm doing it all wrong.

And Thea isn't going to be happy when she sees me with Paisley.

Paisley's phone buzzes incessantly in her pocket.

She grabs for it and reads the screen.

"What's so interesting?" I ask, trying to get a look at the screen.

"Nothing," she says, pulling it close to her body.

"Whatever," I say, turning to go back to my mom and sister.

"You lucked out that we didn't have work this morning."

I'm suddenly annoyed.

"Is your mom okay?" she asks.

I pull up short and turn around to look at her. I try to meter my response.

"I hope so."

-PAISLEY-

He gulps hard a few times.

It's pretty obvious by his body language that I'm the last person he wants to talk to about this, but I had to ask. It felt wrong not to ask. And now, I feel sympathy. Honest to goodness concern. How will I ever finish my revenge scheme if I start feeling *feelings* for Carter?

"She's okay. Right now. She was in the hospital last night, and I really wanted to be there."

"I'm sorry she's sick," I say.

"She's getting better. This was a minor setback."

"Carter?"

"What?" he asks; his whole body is tired.

"I really am sorry about your mom. That sucks. Sincerely."

"Thanks."

We end up walking to the front of the store together, because really, I have what I need and I don't want to get arrested for extended lurking or something.

I get in line behind his mom and sister, who are almost done paying.

Carter introduces us.

His sister's face remains stony, but his mom's breaks into a wide grin.

"Why, Paisley, I remember you from back in the day. You were always so mischievous," she says. "Always up to something."

"I still am," I say. I know she thinks I'm joking because she laughs, but I feel a little bad given the source toward which my mischief flows these days.

"We'll give you a ride back to campus," she says.

Thea doesn't look pleased.

"Oh no, I'm fine. I don't mind the walk."

"But it's pouring," Carter's mom insists.

And indeed it is.

It's really hard to say no to a ride in a cold October downpour.

The car ride back to the dorm is quiet. I thank Thea as I get out of the car but she doesn't say anything back. I say goodbye and I leave Carter to say goodbye and potentially complain more about me to his sister.

The elevator takes eight million years to come, so I'm still standing there with soggy bags when Carter walks past on the way to his room.

"So I guess your sister hates me. Makes sense that you would talk to her about this stuff. She seems like she'd be a good person to talk to," I say, keeping my tone breezy.

"Yeah, pretty much. You don't make a very good impression when I tell stories about you."

"Oh, I'm sure," I say. "But even if everyone in your family hates me, I really do hope the best for your mom. Let me know how it goes for her."

He stops and shakes his head. "Listen, Paisley. I don't need your pity. You've made it pretty clear that you don't like me. I definitely don't have any interest in keeping you updated on my mom's health."

"Okay," I say, wishing I had some retort. Why do I feel so disheartened? This is what I've wanted him to say all along.

"We're not friends. This isn't going to make us friends."

I kind of hate that he's saying this. It's making me sad. But I hate being sad, so instead I get angry.

"I wasn't trying to be friends," I say. "I was trying to be decent about someone who has cancer."

"Too little, too late," he says.

He's about to walk away, but I call to him, "Oh, Carter.

By the way, since you missed calc this morning, you should know that class is canceled on Thursday."

"Sure, thanks for the message," he says even though he doesn't sound grateful at all.

I walk away slowly, imagining that I'm an action movie star casually walking away from an exploding bomb behind me.

This is my ultimate revenge.

I know I promised Stef that I wouldn't play any pranks involving class. But this is my last one. I just need to get it out of my system.

Later on that evening, Stef is at class and I take an early shower and climb into bed. I spent the afternoon making T-shirts and not thinking about Carter, so I deserve the evening off.

I decide to call my mom because while I've been very busy not thinking about Carter, I have been thinking about moms in general and my mom in particular.

"Hey, Mom," I say.

"Hey, Paisley, sweetheart. Are you okay?"

"Just missing you," I tell her.

"Well, it's awfully nice to hear your voice."

"It's nice to hear yours too."

"So what's up, buttercup?"

"I was thinking about moms. I saw Carter's mom today," I tell her. I'd previously told her all my Carter issues, minus the part with the making out. She doesn't need to know that part.

"Stacy. I remember her. She was always trying to get

me involved with class stuff and PTA, but I was so busy back then with night school. I wish I could have been more present back then. Especially since she was so welcoming."

"Yeah. I always liked her. But she's sick. And I guess I forget sometimes that moms can get sick. Like, really sick. It made me want to check on you."

"Oh, honey, I'm fine. You know that, right?"

"And you'd tell me if you weren't?"

"Yes."

"Pinkie swear?"

"Cross my heart."

"Please don't hope to die," I say.

"Cross my heart and hope to live. Anyway, I'm a nurse. I'm very aware of my own health."

"I know." My eyes prick with tears so I decide to change the subject. "How's your alone time going?"

"Well, you know. It's funny you should ask. It's a little boring. I miss my binge-watching buddy."

"Oh yeah? What are you watching?"

"Parks and Recreation."

"Well it's about damn time, Mother."

She laughs and we continue to talk. I feel better. I feel like this is what I needed even though I didn't necessarily know it before I called. I needed to talk to her. I was missing her. But even more than that, I was missing our time together. I was missing *us.*

We hang up a few minutes later, and I remind myself I could go see her anytime.

But work and school and selling T-shirts and trying to

get in even a little bit of socializing all take too much time. I need to prioritize.

I fall asleep thinking about priorities.

I fall asleep thinking that I need to be better about Carter. Not nicer to him, I don't owe him that, but the universe seems to be getting some kind of revenge on him. Maybe I don't need to be in charge of his retribution. Maybe that's not my place.

I'm not changing my mind about him because his mom is sick. That's not what this is about. I'm not changing my mind about him at all.

But maybe I don't have to give him a hard time.

Maybe lying to him about calc can be my final act of Paisley justice.

Maybe I don't have to make things more difficult for him.

Maybe it's time to move on.

CHAPTER FOURTEEN

-CARTER-

On Thursday, by some gift from a higher power, Paisley and I don't have work together. I'm not sure what I would do. I don't think I could handle dealing with her so soon after her learning about my mom.

I've been thinking about transferring.

It's a thought that's gone through my head a couple of times lately. I could go to school someplace closer to where my mom and Thea live. Just live at home, save some money. It would be better for everyone.

On the other hand, it's not like I would get away from Paisley so easily. Thea just happened to buy a house in the town next to where Paisley lives, where I lived up until middle school. I'd definitely end up seeing her around still. Because I'm lucky like that.

I go to my other classes, ignoring Paisley. Thea's advice plays over and over in my head. It's time to get over her, over this.

It's not like it's difficult. We're not friends. We were only ever maybe friends in my head. And even that didn't last for a full forty-eight hours, and it didn't exactly get off on the right foot for platonic friendship anyway.

I really need to stop thinking about her. And the first weekend of school. And everything that's wrong with my life.

And that kiss.

But how do you start fresh with your life in the last week of October?

Maybe I could pretend that Halloween is the start of a new me.

A better Carter.

Maybe I could convince myself.

When I get home after dinner, I check my email and I have a message from my calc TA, Becca. It reads:

> Carter,
> You've missed two classes in a row and today there was a pop quiz. Your grade was already suffering. This string of missed classes is not going to help. I hate to see someone give up like this. You've worked hard this semester, and I don't want you to lose your momentum.

It goes on from there, giving me options and possibilities for making up the work, but that my grade on the pop quiz will remain a zero.

I don't understand what happened.

I start to write an email back, explaining that I don't know what happened.

But then I realize. I do know what happened. I know exactly what happened.

I'm so embarrassed and angry. Why would I listen to her? Why would I fall for this trick? Why would she do this in the first place? What does she stand to gain from making my life worse and harder?

I run up to her room. She better be home because I need to confront her while I'm angry. I can't wait for this feeling to dissipate. I can't sleep on it. I need to act. I know this is her fault and I need to hear it from her.

I fly up the stairs two at a time, bursting through the doorway into her hallway, and race down the hall, nearly knocking into someone coming out of the bathroom. I barely stop to apologize.

And then I'm there, standing in front of her door.

I pound on it.

-PAISLEY-

Someone is pounding on my door. I'm almost a little scared to open it since Stef isn't home. What if it's a mass murderer?

But also, how would Stef protect me from a mass murderer? Sometimes my thought process makes no sense.

I creep over to the door, not wanting to alert the door-pounding mass murderer to the fact that I'm in here alone. I lean into the peephole, and there out in the hallway is Carter.

He's sweaty and red in the face and can barely catch his breath.

He's terrifying.

I don't want to talk to him when he's like this. Mostly because it can mean only one thing. He knows I lied about calculus.

I was going to come clean to him because we ended up having a pop quiz. And I wasn't trying to ruin his grade or make him fail. I don't know what I was doing. I was going to be a better Paisley! At least, that's what I thought on Tuesday night. But then I haven't really seen him and I didn't want to bring it up.

I take a deep breath and open the door.

He pushes through and stands in the middle of my room. He spins in a circle, taking in the mess that my room is. I'm in the midst of catching up on orders. I don't know who Zoe promoted my T-shirts to, but I have been overwhelmed. I have the urge to hide my wares, lest Carter say something else disparaging about them.

Carter brushes his sweaty hair off his forehead. He actually looks kind of hot and that thought makes me hate myself.

"Why?" he asks, his voice oddly, suspiciously calm. I get goose bumps.

"Why?" I respond. "Why what?"

"Why would you do that, Paisley?"

"Do what?" Maybe if I play coy and oblivious long enough, a mass murderer will eventually come along and finish us off.

He massages his temples.

I know I'm in the wrong here. I know that this is what

being a bad person looks like. But I don't know what to do about it. I don't know what my recourse is.

"Please, Paisley," he says. "No more games. I'm so tired of games. I don't know why you decided to use me as a plaything this semester. I suppose it's because I made myself vulnerable to you. But, like. This? This is disgusting."

I throw my arms up and shake my head.

"Honestly, I have no recourse or excuse," I say. My thoughts bursting from my mouth like I have no filter. "I was pissed off at you. I didn't like what you were saying. I didn't want to hear it. I wanted to get back at you in some small way. I didn't think you'd actually believe me."

"That's ridiculous. Why wouldn't I believe you?"

"Gee. I don't know, because I've been a complete bitch to you."

"See, you've been a pain in the ass. You haven't been friendly or kind or made any attempt to even act neutrally toward me. But I didn't think you would downright try to make me fail a class. Try to mess with my grades. Try to ruin my semester with some weird passive-aggressive shit because of something I did when I was twelve."

"Well, I did," I say, sticking out my chin defiantly. "Why wouldn't you believe it? Why wouldn't you believe I was capable of that?"

He runs his hands through his hair again and tugs at the ends, making it stick up in every direction. "I was a kid, Paisley. I was a child. Didn't you make mistakes when you were in middle school?"

"I didn't flush anybody's gym clothes if that's what you're asking."

"Don't you have any feelings? Don't you understand that I'm just barely surviving here? I'm barely making it through? And you're doing everything you can to make me miserable. To punish me for something I did to someone else a million years ago? You act like you're so interested in fairness and loyalty and all that bullshit. But really, you're out here for you. Because you enjoy having the power."

"Oh my god," I say. "Where do you come up with this garbage?" It's not my best move, lashing out like this. But he's just. He's right about everything and I have no arguments. Nothing left. Not a leg to stand on.

He shakes his head. "You're not even going to try to apologize."

"I'm sorry I told you that calc was canceled. I'll do my best to fix it."

He narrows his eyes at me. "I have a scholarship you know? I have a GPA I need to maintain. This isn't a game. This is my life. This is my future. And you're out here manipulating it, trying to ruin it. Why? Why are you doing this?"

I have so many reasons and I can't think of even one right now. They all sound like weak excuses compared to the big angry scene he's making. He's so full of logic, and I'm over here like, "Because you're not nice!"

But the problem is, he is nice. He's the nicest boy on earth, and I've managed to piss him off so hard he'll never even want to look at me ever again.

I need to say something.

"It'll be okay," I say.

"No. It really won't be." He looks around the room,

taking in everything that I'm working on. He huffs out a breath and shakes his head. I almost think he's going to start throwing things.

Instead, he walks purposefully from my room and slams the door behind him. I'm not sure I've ever felt so awful in my entire life.

-CARTER-

I go back to my room but can't concentrate on anything. I should really email back my TA and try to plead my case. But where will that get me? It's a bunch of "he said, she said" crap. I'm going to look like a joke, like an immature asshole, just because I was involved in this situation. Paisley has never and will never see me as anything besides a bully that needs to be taken down. And that's fine, that's her problem. Unfortunately, she also made it my problem now.

I will figure this out.

But maybe right now isn't the best time. Maybe right now I need to take a beat, walk away, distract myself.

Ray comes in then and I vent to him, telling him the whole story, every little detail, right down to the T-shirts Paisley was making when I walked into her room.

"Wait, what?" Ray asks, interrupting me.

"T-shirts. She makes T-shirts in her dorm room and sells them online."

Ray's whole face brightens.

"You want to get back at her?"

"More than anything in the world."

"I have a great idea."

He scrounges into his bottom drawer and pulls out a student handbook.

"Did we all get those?" I ask.

He shrugs. "I don't know, I found it in my desk." Upon further inspection, it has last year's dates in it, so maybe they stopped handing them out. "But I have this habit of reading pretty much everything I can."

"Because you like to be a know-it-all," I say with a grin.

"Well, yeah, you don't get to be a *Jeopardy!* teen tournament champion by not being a know-it-all."

"True."

He flips to the index and then finds the right page and hands me the book, pointing at a list. I read out loud.

"Solicitation, collecting money, and/or selling items under any circumstances within a residence hall is prohibited. Students who break this rule will be required to cease all sales immediately. If they do not obey the initial warning, they will be placed on housing probation."

I laugh for what feels like the first time in days.

"So, who do we report her to?" Ray asks.

"Anyone? Everyone?"

"Let's get to work."

-PAISLEY-

I sent Becca, the calc TA, an email last night about needing to see her today. I need to come clean. This whole situation is bad for my karma.

And my complexion. I woke up with a zit the size of the moon on my forehead today.

We make plans to meet late Friday afternoon. The campus is nearly deserted at this point. Which is good. I don't need anyone to hear me groveling on behalf of my worst enemy. But I need to make this one up. I need to solve this one.

Because as much as it pains me to admit it, Carter is right. I'm punishing him for something he did a long time ago and it's not exactly a case where the punishment fits the crime. He shouldn't lose his scholarship because I'm pissed off on Henry's behalf. Henry would hate that. And that's just one reason, in a sea of endless reasons, to make it right.

As we take seats in her teeny, tiny office, I realize I hope this meeting takes a long time. Because when it's over, I need to go home and face the music of my overwhelming T-shirt orders. The other day, one of the girls on my floor showed up in my room begging for the T-shirt she ordered. It's getting to be way too much.

"So what's up?" Becca asks.

I explain the best I can what happened with Carter. How I told him class was canceled. How I have this silly vendetta against him. That I didn't think he would believe me. Even as the words come out of my mouth, I can't believe that I did this. I can't believe that I'm here admitting it.

"You guys are first years, right?" Becca asks.

"Yeah."

"You have some growing up to do."

"I know. I was wrong. It's such a long story and it goes back such a long time. I really didn't think he'd trust me to give him that message. I figured he'd at least check with someone else or realize that if class was canceled there'd be an email about it, not just an announcement."

She shakes her head, and I can feel the disappointment rolling off her.

"I'm not here to babysit. I have zero interest in your shenanigans. But if you really did this to him, and you want to take responsibility, then my offer is give him your grade on the pop quiz and you get a zero."

"Okay," I say.

"But, Paisley, he missed class twice this week. You can't take responsibility for both classes. He hasn't turned in homework in a week. He hasn't been participating. I shouldn't even be talking to you about this."

"Then why are you?"

"Because my point is, he's not doing well on his own. I'd hate for you to ruin your grade for his."

"Nope. It's my fault."

"Him missing two classes isn't your fault. He still missed Tuesday."

"He had a family emergency," I say.

"Well then, he should have come in to see me. Or emailed. Or done something for himself. Why isn't he here?"

"Because he hates excuses."

"Well, they're the only way to get excused," she says.

I nod.

"I should report you to the dean's office, but I'm going to let you off this time. Don't make me regret it."

"I won't," I promise.

I don't leave feeling much better than I did when I got there, but I did what I could.

Now to tell Carter that he got a ninety-eight on the pop quiz. At least I have some good news for him. For once.

That is, if he's even willing to see me.

CHAPTER FIFTEEN

-CARTER-

At work on Saturday morning, Paisley is waiting with two big cups of Starbucks. She sprang for the good stuff.

"I don't want to be friends and I don't accept the coffee," I say pushing past her and into the building.

"I'm not going to beg. But I'm also going to make you drink this coffee because I got your favorite and I don't like it."

"How do you know what my favorite is?"

"I heard what you ordered on Employee Appreciation Day," I say, feeling more than a little sheepish. I was mostly listening because I had considered putting something in his drink. Like a laxative. Or a bug.

"It's a four-pump mocha with an extra shot?"

"It is. Even though I think it both smells and tastes like burnt rubber."

I take the cup from her. I can't help it. I am weak for that burnt rubber flavor.

We settle in, and it's a quiet Saturday morning. It's gorgeous outside. The leaves are changing color at an alarming rate all of a sudden. One day they were all dull green and the next they were a cacophony of red and yellow and orange.

I take a sip of my mocha and get started on my homework.

"Please let me help you with calc," Paisley says about halfway through our shift. She's peering over my shoulder, watching me work.

I stare down at the page. "Did I do something wrong?"

"Carter, this whole page is a mess," she says, gesturing at one of the problems I was working on.

"You only feel bad for me because of my mom. You pity me."

"If it was pity because of your mom, I wouldn't have told you calc was canceled. You can trust me because I was a bitch to you even after I found out there was a reason to pity you."

"Your logic is super flawed." But there's a change in the air today, and I don't know what it is. Maybe it's the catharsis of ratting her out to student housing, which she doesn't seem to know about yet. Or maybe it's something she put in my mocha, but I feel a little more . . . warmly toward her than I have recently.

"Listen, I don't feel bad for you. I feel guilty because I was a total bitch and I need to make up some karma points. And clear up my skin." She lifts her bangs and shows me the largest, reddest, angriest zit I've ever seen.

"I'm pretty sure that zit is karma at work," I say, staring at it. I swear it's pulsing.

"So I went to our calc TA," she says. "And she said she'd give you my grade on the pop quiz. Congrats on your ninety-eight."

"Best damn grade I've gotten this semester," I mutter.

"See? You're not doing well. Just let me help you."

"I'm doing fine," I say. I feel defensive. I don't need her knowing about my weaknesses.

"But are you?"

"I'm managing."

"But just maybe you could use some help."

"Probably not."

"Maybe I'm doing really, really well in calculus. Maybe I'm like a bit of a calc genius and could help you out before the exam next week. Give you tips. Show you the error of your ways."

Does she already know about the complaint and she's trying to lure me into getting tutored so she can screw with my grade that way?

But then why go to the trouble of talking to our TA?

"I like everything but the last thing you said. I don't need you to make me feel bad about not being good at math on top of everything else you've done."

I don't love the direction this conversation is going but I also really do need help. And whether I like it or not, Paisley owes me. Which reminds me.

"What do you get out of this?" I ask. Because whether

she owes me or not, I'm having a hard time believing that she's doing this out of the goodness of her heart.

-PAISLEY-

"Well, quite frankly, I found out that Brightly tests almost exclusively off class notes and I've noticed you taking copious notes. Maybe you could share those with me?" It only just occurred to me in this moment. I never got around to making a friend in U.S. history and I'm really not the expert I thought I was.

"Maybe," he says, but I can tell he's thinking about this too hard.

"I promise I'm not trying to make you feel bad about not being good at math," I say, rolling my eyes. "But I know I can help you, and it seems like you can help me with Brightly's class."

He rubs his temples. "Yeah, sure. I could use all the help I can get."

We make a plan to meet up at the library on Monday night. At least we don't have any work or classes together between now and then so it's not like I have to see him over and over.

On Monday afternoon, I'm wasting time in my room when I notice I have an email from my resident advisor, Kenny. He says he needs to meet up with me at my earliest convenience. I respond that we can talk now.

When I open the door, Kenny is already standing there, looking stressed out.

"Hey," I say. "What's up?"

"Oh, yeah, Paisley. Hi." He looks up at me and then back down on the paper in his hands. "So you've had a complaint made against you?"

"I have?" He sounds so confused.

"Yeah, apparently you've been running a business out of your dorm room? That's not allowed."

"Oh," I say, a little surprised. "I've been making T-shirts for other students but I didn't realize that's considered a business."

"Yeah," he says.

"Am I getting fined or something?"

"Not unless you continue to work out of your dorm room after this warning."

"Okay," I say. I want to ask questions, but I don't want to get myself in more trouble later. Like, I'm sure I can sell off my inventory pretty quick, making sure I fulfill all the orders, but that doesn't seem like something I need to mention to Kenny.

"So, yeah, okay," Kenny says, running a hand through his hair and making it stand on end.

"Can you tell me who made the complaint?"

He shakes his head. "I couldn't tell you even if I was allowed. It was made anonymously."

I nod. I have a feeling I know who would make an anonymous complaint. And it's certainly none of the people who bought my T-shirts. I suppose it could be Stef, but she was so supportive.

I head over to the student center to work on homework for a while, and on my way to meet Carter, I pick up some food for us. I just need to make things right. I need to make things better.

I text Stef.

Paisley: Kenny told me I can't sell T-shirts from the room anymore.

Stef: What?!? Why??

Paisley: Someone complained about it.

Stef: WHO?!?!?! Everyone loves your T-shirts.

Paisley: My money is on Carter.

Stef: OMG. I will beat him up for you. What are you going to do?

Paisley: Nothing. This is it. I'll allow this last act of revenge and the war can be over.

Stef: Wow. End of an era. We'll have to discuss this further in person. When are you coming home? Want to get dinner with me?

Paisley: Well, um. I'm actually meeting up with (gulp) Carter.

Stef: I'm sorry. BUT WTF???

Paisley: It's all part of my "getting over" the prank war.

Stef: Are you being held hostage? Is he blackmailing you?

Paisley: It's a long story. But I kind of set him up to fail a calc quiz so now I'm helping him. It's about karma.

Stef: It's about guilt.

Paisley: That too.

Stef: Well. Have fun. I guess. Are you going to be able to get through this?

Paisley: I should be okay. Thank you for your concern.

-CARTER-

I know that the only reason Paisley offered to help me is because she feels bad about my mom. And also because of the other multitude of sins she's committed this semester. But who's counting.

I'm not sure I can tell the difference between sympathy and pity though, and in this case, I don't want to. I don't care if she's only helping me because she pities me because quite frankly, I really need the help.

I could have gone to the tutoring center, but that felt an awful lot like admitting defeat. The longer I didn't go, the harder it was to convince myself to get help. There's a pretty solid chance that I would have failed the exam next week if Paisley hadn't offered to tutor me.

Also, the idea of transferring or even dropping out altogether was starting to sound better and better.

So really, she's saving me a lot of trouble.

Or hopefully she is. There's still the chance that she's not as good at calculus as she claims to be and I'll fail no matter what. On the other hand, maybe she's trying to further sabotage my grades. Anything is possible.

But I also kind of like to imagine that maybe she's feeling just a little bit of remorse about everything. That would be great. It'd be nice to know that she's not a sociopath and that she can actually feel emotions for other people. But I'm trying not to get my hopes too high.

The plan is to meet at the library. I wait out front for her on one of the stone benches. The seat is cold under me, but it feels like it's the only thing keeping me awake. All these five-thirty wake-up calls are catching up with me.

When she walks up, she has takeout containers with her.

"I know you like the fries from the student center so I brought you some. There's also a grilled cheese or a chicken sandwich. Your choice. I'll take whatever you don't want."

I grab the grilled cheese. This is quite the unexpected turn of events. I don't even really know what to say to her.

"Thanks for the food," I say, finally deciding to keep it simple. "And the help. Though I'm not sure how much you're really going to be able to help. Math isn't exactly my strong suit." I shove a bunch of fries in my mouth to keep from saying anything else. I need to stop making myself so vulnerable around Paisley; she'll just use it against me.

"Math wasn't my strong suit until Henry started helping me," she says, staring me right in the eye.

I blink first.

"Did you bring any ketchup?" I ask.

She pulls some packets out of the bag.

"I'm going to help you *ketchup* with math," she says as she sprinkles the packets on the bench between us.

I look over at her and she has this huge grin on her face, like I could probably count all her teeth.

"Oh my god," I say. "That's a terrible pun."

She snorts a laugh.

And then I snort a laugh.

And then we're both laughing so hard we can't even eat.

"Why are we laughing?" she asks.

"I don't know."

"It was something about your face. The face you made."

"But it was your face!" I say.

We finish eating, but it takes a while because we keep bursting out into laughter every minute or two.

"How will I ever ketchup with you?" I ask as we put our garbage in the trash can.

"You mustard hard?" she says.

"Are you having a stroke?"

"No, that sentence didn't work out the way I wanted it to. You must work hard."

"Yeah, it obviously got away from you because that was nonsense word salad."

"Mayonnaise? Something about mayonnaise?"

"I think you're addicted to condiment puns," I say, pulling the door open and holding it for her to step through.

We find a quiet spot up in the stacks. There aren't too many people around, probably because it's still basically dinnertime. The dining hall is likely packed right now.

We set up the work we need to do, but every few minutes one of us will mention a condiment and the other will start laughing.

"Horseradish?" I ask. "Is there something there?"

"Now you're flat-out mocking me."

We do get some actual work done. I might even not fail the test next week.

We work for hours actually, and I'm surprised when I look up and the clock says it's after ten.

"Time flies when you're making puns," Paisley says when she sees me glancing at the clock.

I shake my head. "You're the worst."

"Bad puns make me happy. I'm going to start screen-printing puns on T-shirts. I'm definitely going to have to make one that says 'time flies when you're making puns.' Heck I might have to even rename my Etsy shop."

"You still have one of those?" I ask. "I thought—" But I don't let myself finish that sentence.

"Well, actually. I got in trouble with my RA about selling stuff out of my dorm room. I'm not allowed to actually make any more T-shirts to sell while I live on campus, and I'm not technically supposed to take any money from people. But there's no reason I can't do it online. I'll just do it from home. Over breaks and stuff."

I hum a response and hope for the subject to drop.

She narrows her eyes at me. She must realize how uncomfortable I am.

"I know you know, Carter," she says simply.

"I may have been the one to report you," I say, not looking at her.

"Thanks for confessing."

I glance over at her, and she's playing with the string on her hoodie.

She clears her throat. "Maybe that makes us even."

-PAISLEY-

It's weird that I'm not even all that pissed off at Carter for telling on me. The whole T-shirt operation was getting sort of overwhelming. People were coming up to me all over campus, asking me when they would get their orders. I don't even know how they knew I was the one making them.

Anyway, karma's a bitch and I have to accept it.

And really, it does feel like Carter and I are even now. That's something.

We work hard for another few minutes, and then Carter leans back in his chair and throws his pencil down.

"I need caffeine or sugar or something," he says.

"There's a little room with a vending machine down-stairs. I feel like I've gotten obsessed with vending machines in college. I don't think I ever thought much about them before. But they're everywhere here. And provide me with most of my sustenance."

"I know. And so convenient."

"Too convenient."

We clean up our stuff and wander downstairs, making our way through the main study area. But before we make it to the vending machine, an announcement is made that the library is closing.

-CARTER-

"I guess we should head back to the dorm," I say.

"We could work more when we get back there," she offers. "If you have any more questions."

"Maybe."

I suck in a deep breath.

"Are you only doing this because you feel bad for me?" I ask.

She shrugs, her little half shrug that I used to find so endearing.

"No. Yes. Maybe. I don't know?"

"Will I ever be able to get on your good side? Or even your neutral side?" I ask. We're walking slowly back to the dorm even though it's pretty cold out and she doesn't have a jacket. "Especially now that you know I foiled your T-shirt business?"

She pulls her hoodie tighter around her as the wind gusts through the trees. "Yeah, I think so."

"Is there something I can do?" I ask. "I'm serious."

"You could apologize to Henry."

"I did," I say.

"What? When? Why haven't I heard about it?"

"I sent him a message on Facebook."

She snorts. "My Henry Lai doesn't have Facebook. So you apologized to some random Korean kid named Henry Lai. Did they write back?"

"No," I say, scowling at the ground. "To be fair, I haven't seen him in four years. But oh man. I swear I tried. I could show you the message."

She's laughing, whether at me or at the situation or something completely different, it's hard to tell.

"I'll give you that," she says. "You tried. No denying it."

We're almost at the dorm now, and I know there are other things I want to say to her, other topics I want to broach. This is the first time since before she found out who I really was that I've felt like I had her attention, like I might be able to say something and make her listen.

"I really am sorry about all that stuff," I say. It's an incomplete thought and an imperfect saying but it's the best I can do at the moment. "About the middle school stuff and about what I did the first weekend of school."

"I'm sorry about everything I've done this semester," she says.

"I accept your apology." I wait a beat. "Do you accept mine?"

"Yeah, I'm almost there. It's just, you were a dick. You were a real dick back then. You were so into making life miserable for Henry. And it felt like there was nothing anyone could do about it."

"I always expected him to tell on me."

"That's not like Henry," she says. "He would never dream of it. He flies under the radar. All he wants is for people to leave him alone."

"Where is he? Where's he go to college?"

"Penn State. He's going to be an engineer of course. I tried to convince him to go here, but he really wanted to go farther away. He had his eyes on Boston, but Penn gave him more money."

"Good for him," I say. And I mean it. "I didn't let myself think too much about him over the years. I did feel guilty."

"Well, at least you're not a sociopath."

I have to laugh since that's the word I used for her earlier. But I decide against mentioning it, mostly because I'm not prepared to feel her wrath. It's too nice to just talk to her.

We're nearly at the dorm now and I'm running out of steam.

She slides her key card and lets us in. We head for the stairs.

"Thanks again for helping me."

"You're welcome again," she says as we get to the second-floor landing.

"You didn't actually say you're welcome earlier," I point out.

"Well then, you're welcome now. Seriously. Anytime. I'm happy to help. Nobody deserves to fail calculus."

"Not even me?" I ask.

"Not even you, Farter."

I laugh. "Night, Parsley."

"Night."

And then she's gone, through the door to the stairs. I watch her through the little window. Before she starts to ascend, she looks back. I can't tell if she can see me, but I like knowing that she looked back.

CHAPTER SIXTEEN

-PAISLEY-

It's Halloween and I'm stuck at work. I get all the worst shifts anyway, so it's not like I'm shocked. I guess I'm mostly shocked that Carter isn't here with me. Misery loves company and all that. Instead I'm on with a guy named Derek whom I'd never met before, and he's spent most of the very quiet shift hitting on one of the girls who works in the weight area.

The good news is that at least Carter and I are getting a break from each other. The bad news is that I think I might actually miss him. That's really bad news. Our little jaunt to the library was already a week ago, and between work and class, I've seen him almost every day since. You'd think I'd want a break. I may or may not have had a fairly illicit dream about his lips three nights in a row.

Or maybe I just miss having someone to sit at the desk with.

Yeah, that's probably it.

I try to make eye contact with my desk mate, but Derek is really good at avoiding eye contact when he wants to.

I could use a bathroom break, and even though it's super quiet, I know I shouldn't leave the desk completely unattended.

So I wait.

I consider my options. I could page Derek back to the desk. I could go into the weight room and ask him to cover the desk for a few minutes. That thing could happen where sometimes you suddenly just don't have to pee anymore. I could take my chances and run to the bathroom, leaving the desk unattended.

I decide to text my friends.

Starting with Lizzie. But it turns out she's currently in Ohio seeing her boyfriend Cameron, and I don't want to interrupt them. Not for my silly complaints. They don't deserve that.

I text Madison, but her only response is to send me a mirror selfie of her dressed as Wonder Woman.

I text Henry, but all he wants to do is complain about people being loud in his hallway while he's trying to study for an organic chemistry test he has next week.

I check the clock. It's still only nine thirty.

This night is so boring it might drag on forever. I don't know why the gym would bother staying open until eleven on Halloween night when everyone is obviously out partying. Although there's a guy here on the treadmill wearing a dinosaur mask, so that's fun. Should I stop him? Is that unsafe? It seems like he might not be able to see very well.

Paisley: There's a guy on the treadmill wearing a Tyrannosaurus rex mask. Do you think I should talk to him?

Henry: I wish I had a Tyrannosaurus rex mask.

Paisley: That wasn't the question.

Henry: Maybe? I don't know. I gave up on studying, and I'm going to a Halloween party that the Society of Asian American Engineers is throwing.

Paisley: Do I have the wrong number? Who is this, really?

Henry: Haha. So funny.

Paisley: Who's being funny? I'm legitimately confused/concerned. You. Henry. Are going to a party?

Henry: Might as well. I'm not going to get any work done.

Paisley: Are you going to dress up?

Henry: One of the girls in my hall is loaning me her soccer uniform. So I'm going as a female World Cup soccer winner or something.

Paisley: I don't understand anything that's happening. I think my phone is broken. Or maybe it's suddenly able to text with people in alternate universes. This can't be Henry Lai that I'm talking to. My Henry Lai doesn't dress up and go to Halloween parties. And why a female soccer player?

Henry: Why not? And also, she's the only one who's around who had an idea when I asked if I could borrow something. I look cute in these shorts.

Paisley: WHO ARE YOU AND WHAT HAVE YOU DONE TO MY FRIEND.

Henry: Do you want to see a picture?

Paisley: I honestly can't imagine anything I want more in this world, Henry.

-CARTER-

It's Halloween and I should have plans. Ray even invited me to the party his brother is throwing. I kind of lied and told him that I needed to do homework. I'll make it up to him.

It's not a complete lie. I do need to get homework done. The thing is, I could have easily gotten it done before going out.

And instead of doing anything productive, I'm thinking about Paisley. Wondering what she's up to tonight. I know she had to work.

Maybe I should casually stop by. I know they're showing the original *Halloween* at midnight in the field behind the fitness center. It's going to be cold, but there's something so creepy about an outdoor movie on Halloween.

Maybe she'd be into it?

For the first time ever, I wish I had her cell phone number.

What if I get over to the fitness center and she's her usual "ew, Carter" self? I need a cover. I grab my history notes. I never got around to giving them to her. That's a better excuse than anything else I can come up with.

Why does everything have to be so hard?

I look in the mirror and try to pump myself up.

"You can do this. You blew off Ray to do this. So you gotta suck it up and try."

What am I going to tell Ray if he realizes that I'm not home studying?

I shrug. That's something for Future Carter to worry about.

I grab a coat and, at the last second, a sheet to sit on. Even if Paisley doesn't want to see the movie, maybe I'll go by myself.

I head out the door into the cool, breezy night.

-PAISLEY-

I hear the door open and someone stands at the desk clearing their throat. I can't believe I'm being interrupted right in the middle of the most amazing conversation I have ever had. With anyone. Ever. I need to see Henry dressed up for Halloween. But I also need to do my job.

I look up and it's Carter. He's smiling. A lot.

"I'm very surprised to see you here," I say, putting my phone facedown on the desk. I want to be able to bask in the glory of the picture when it comes later and not get a spoiler from the little thumbnail on my lock screen.

"I, um," he starts. Then he chews his lip. "I brought you my history notes."

"Really?" I ask. "On Halloween?"

He hands them to me and I flip through them. "These are really good notes." I look up at him. "How did you get so good at taking notes?"

He blushes. "My mom made me go to this tutoring place after school freshman year. Like every day after school for a month I took a class on study skills. They taught us how to take notes."

"I feel like I should take a study skills class now. Do they let college kids into those classes?"

He grins. "I'm not sure."

I flip through the pages again. "It'd probably be worth looking into," I mutter.

"Is anyone here with you?" he asks, changing the subject.

I explain about Derek and the super quiet night. Then we watch the T. rex on the treadmill for a minute.

"He's really going for it," Carter says.

"He really is."

Carter takes his usual seat next to me and a weird, jittery feeling in my chest seems to settle, like things are finally the way they're supposed to be.

"Don't you have somewhere you need to be tonight?" I ask, leaning back in my chair.

He shrugs. "I was thinking about going to see a scary movie. They're showing *Halloween* out on the lawn behind here at midnight."

"By yourself?"

"I don't know. I thought maybe you'd want to come."

"Why?"

-CARTER-

I was actually prepared for this question. I figured pretty much anything I asked Paisley to do tonight would be met with a question like this.

I suck in a deep breath.

"Just seems like something friends do," I say.

She nods. "If we're going to be friends, I think I need to know a few things first."

"You know, I had the biggest crush on you back then," I say. That's probably not what she was wondering about, but it seems like something I want her to know.

"Well, that can't be true. Twelve-year-old Paisley spit when she talked, had permanent halitosis, and the same approximate temperament as a honey badger."

I shrug. "Well, you've changed a little, sure. We all have."

"But have you really?" she asks.

"Oh, come on, Paisley. I'm a changed man from middle school. You can see that, right? That I've grown up? I thought we went through this all the other night on our walk back from the library."

She sighs. "I don't understand why of all the people you could pick on, you would pick on Henry. He was just trying to make it through the day without a panic attack. Maybe if you explain what happened? I can't imagine Henry provoking you, but . . ." She shrugs and lets the thought trail off.

"I guess I lashed out. I felt threatened and I needed to take it out on him. It's hard to feel vulnerable."

"Wait, what?"

I shrug. "I don't like feeling vulnerable."

"No, no. The part about feeling threatened by Henry. What would Henry do that would make you feel threatened?"

"You don't know? He never told you what happened?"

"Um, no. Definitely not."

"Oh. Well, that's unexpected. So, seventh grade was rough. I hate excuses so I won't go into the details, but I was having a lot of family issues."

"That can be rough," she says.

"It was. And I was crying in the bathroom one day. And Henry walked in. He was really nice about it, of course. He honestly made me feel better. But in that moment, I was so scared that people would find out that I was crying at school, I told him he better never tell anyone."

"That's ridiculous; Henry would never tell anyone anything."

"I didn't know that. And as a twelve-year-old, I was terrified. Everything was already the worst. School was the one place that remained okay and untouched. I couldn't risk it."

"So he saw you cry once and you decided to make his life miserable?"

"Well, no. He walked in on me crying a couple of times. Apparently, we were on a similar bathroom schedule."

"You'd have thought you would have learned to cry elsewhere. And not in public if you were so worried."

"You'd have thought. But I didn't. And it was always Henry walking in. And sometimes, outside of the bathroom, he'd ask me if I was okay. Anytime he'd ask, I would make sure to do something to him. To make him pay."

"To make him pay for being nice to you?"

I lean my elbows on my knees. "Paisley, I'm not saying it was logical. I'm not saying this is an excuse. It's just the story."

She scratches her neck and eyes her phone. It's lying facedown on the desk, and I can tell she's itching to text Henry, to verify my claims.

"I don't know why you would think Henry would tell people about this. He never even told me."

"I just can't believe he never told you. Even after all this time."

"That's how Henry is. He's amazing. Even when I told him that I made out with you, he didn't get mad at me. He's the best friend I could have ever hoped to have."

"So would he really be that upset if we, I don't know, were friends? Were maybe civil to each other? Hung out sometimes when we weren't at work or studying?"

She doesn't respond. She looks away, watching the second hand on the clock above the desk tick away.

When she still doesn't say anything, I continue.

"And after we moved, my mom sent me to a therapist. If that, I don't know, sweetens the pot for you. Because I was aggressive and I had behavioral issues. It helped. Everything helped. And I grew up. I'm different. Though sometimes I still get a little angry."

She stares at me like she's trying to formulate her next thought. She wants to argue with me, I know she does. But I don't think I've left much room for arguing.

The guy in the T. rex mask leaves while I'm thinking. I've probably put Carter through enough. I don't know why I'm even forcing him to say all this. I don't know why I can't just . . . admit that I want to be friends with him.

("Friends or more, friends or more!" a little voice in the back of my head chants. "Kiss him! Kiss him!")

Then Derek comes out from the weight room, interrupting my train of thought.

"The big boss man called and said that if there's no one here at ten o'clock, we can close up and leave."

"Oh," I say. "I don't think there's anyone here."

"Yeah, Chrissa and I are going to check the basketball courts, and the lifeguards say there's no one at the pool. Why don't you guys lock the doors so no one else gets in."

"Sounds good to me," I say.

"And then," Derek adds, turning back, "we're going to this haunted hayride. If you want to come?"

I look over at Carter.

"Would you be pissed if we skipped the movie? I've never actually been on a haunted hayride."

"So does that mean we can be friends?" he asks.

"Yes. Of course."

We tell Derek we'll come and he wanders off to start the closing procedure.

"I know I've said this a couple times now in a bunch of different ways, but for the record, I'm sorry about how I spoke to you after the calc thing," Carter says.

"You really don't have anything to apologize for."

"Yeah, but I like to think that I'm less angry today than I used to be. It's kind of like a twelve-step program, for my rage." He blushes.

"You had every right to yell at me," I say. "I was so way out of line, I couldn't even see the line. And I've been out of line the whole semester. I'm sorry for, like, everything. I can't really be more specific than that because there's way too much. I'd be happy to make a list. Maybe create a spreadsheet."

Carter laughs and my world tips slightly on its axis, righting itself, bringing everything to sharp relief.

-CARTER-

Well, this is a surprising turn of events.

I'm not sure what to expect from this outing with Chrissa and Derek. And it's probably better that way. I'm not a big fan of haunted houses, so I hope I don't start weeping like a baby in the middle of it.

On the way to the hayride, Paisley and I are in the backseat of Chrissa's car and she's laughing at her phone. She tips it toward me.

It's a picture of Henry in a soccer uniform. With pigtails.

Paisley can't stop laughing.

"That's a good look for him."

"It is," she agrees. "Henry isn't usually very silly, so this. It's refreshing." She looks like a proud mama bear.

The good news is that the haunted hayride isn't too terrifying. The even better news is that during one of the jump
scares, Paisley grabs my hand for half a second. She drops it
just as quickly, but her hand was warm and it felt right in
mine.

I think I'll chase that feeling.

CHAPTER SEVENTEEN

-PAISLEY-

I need to talk to Henry.

The next morning I wait until nine because that seems like a not completely ludicrous hour to bug someone. I decide to call him, even though the likelihood of him picking up is slim to none.

I pace in circles while the phone rings. He answers on the third.

"I'm so confused," he says by way of greeting. "Do we talk on the phone now?"

"Yes."

"I don't think so. That doesn't sound like us. I'm going to request that we not do this anymore. Twice in one semester is enough."

I ignore him. "How was the party last night? Was it fun?"

"Well, I don't know. I don't know that it was fun in the strictest sense of the word."

"Is it your issue or was it a bad party?" I ask.

"I think it's a mutual issue."

"Was your TA there?"

"Oh my god, why did I ever tell you about her?"

"Because I'm your friend. So spill it, Henry."

"Yes, she was there." I can practically hear him blush.

"Did you talk to her?"

"Yes."

"Was she nice to you? Why wasn't it an awesome party if you got to talk to your crush?"

"I don't know, Paisley. It's really early in the morning. I got home late. And you're calling me. Forcing me to talk on the phone against my will. I thought there was an emergency."

"Well, I just needed to talk to you about something." I give him the quick and dirty summary of my conversation with Carter. "Why didn't you ever tell me what happened?"

"Because he didn't want anyone to know. And it's not like I'm super into gossip or anything."

"Yeah," I say.

"It makes him a tiny bit more sympathetic, right?" Henry prods.

"Yeah, it does."

"Did that hurt you to admit?"

"Yeah, it did."

Henry chuckles.

"I've gotten to this place where it feels like I want to be friends with him, but I don't know."

"But you're just so stubborn. It's time to get over it. I'm over it. Maybe you should be too."

"Even though on top of everything else, he lied to me about who he was?"

"I mean, that's up to you, whether you want to get over that. But if you're just holding a grudge on my behalf, then it's really, really officially time to stop."

"I hate when you get to be the voice of reason."

"I'm always the voice of reason."

"Then what does that make me?"

"The voice of chaos."

I laugh.

"Go for it, Paisley. This is me giving you the go-ahead."

"Nothing is going to happen, Henry."

"Sure. Whatever you say."

"But, you know, thanks."

We hang up a second later and I lie back in my bed, feeling unburdened. Feeling like something is about to change.

I decide to make myself a T-shirt that says THE LINE WAS A DOT, referring to how far over the line I was with Carter.

It's not exactly an apology T-shirt, but I hope he appreciates it.

-CARTER-

Things are looking up for me. Finally.

A few days after Halloween, everything started getting better. And I'm not entirely sure why. I'm not sure if it was being more open with people in general or just that Paisley and I finally came to an understanding. Or that I started taking responsibility for what was wrong with my life. I don't know exactly what it was, but everything feels better.

About a week into November, I go to office hours for General Psych. It seems like even though I have a decent grade in the class, it can't hurt to find out if there's anything else I could be doing. Especially with the final paper. It feels like the instructions for it require a PhD. The amount of research alone could take months. Or at least it seems that way.

Paisley is in the hallway when I walk out.

"Are you having trouble with this class?" I ask.

"Um, you could say that. I guess I just want a little clarification. About what exactly is expected of us with this final paper."

"Good luck in there. I'm not sure I actually understand it any better than before I went in," I tell her.

"See you at work later?" she asks.

"You know it," I say.

Good thing she mentioned it. I'd almost forgotten that we'd been volunteered by Jordan to act as scorekeepers for the volleyball tournament tonight. From six to midnight. What a wild Friday night.

The only good news is it got us out of working all weekend. I guess Jordan was that desperate for help tonight. I barely remember the last time I got to sleep in on both Saturday and Sunday morning in the same weekend.

It's going to be wonderful.

But first, I have to get through tonight.

-PAISLEY-

When I get to work that night, I'm a little intimidated. Apparently, there are going to be four games going on simultaneously for the next six hours.

"Are we really watching all four games at the same time?" I ask Carter as I sit down next to him at the folding table and chairs.

"I hope not. I'm still not clear on the details, but Jordan will be right back with the scorecards and rules."

Jordan returns and explains that we'll be in charge of keeping the scores organized. Someone will report the scores to us for each game. We need to know which team is on which court at all times. Luckily, they all have pretty clearly marked shirts.

On top of that, one of us will be in charge of announcing each game, calling teams to a certain court, and making sure everything goes in a timely fashion.

"I'll be here too, of course," Jordan concludes. "I'll make sure you know what's happening. But I'll also be refereeing one of the games because three different people called out saying they couldn't make it. You guys are getting major gold stars for being here."

Carter and I high-five and then set to work organizing scorecards.

"I should have brought along a sixty-four pack of crayons," I say. "It would have helped to color code these things."

"I'm pretty sure I saw a variety pack of sharpies in the office last week."

"Well, what are you waiting for?" I ask. "Go get them! We only have six minutes until the games start."

Carter dashes off to grab the markers, and I continue trying to organize things.

"I can't believe how well you two are getting along lately," Jordan says, coming over to lean on the table.

"Yeah, we've put some stuff behind us."

"That's great. I wish you had done it sooner. You two are definitely going to be my dynamic duo from here on out."

"I'm just glad you're not still pissed off about the hand-dying incident," I say.

"Nah, the presentation went well. I'm not sure anyone even noticed. They probably just thought I was really cold."

Carter comes back and hands me the pack of markers. There are colors that match all twelve teams in the tournament, so I start writing the team names with the corresponding marker.

I tell Carter what Jordan said and he laughs.

"I hope 'dynamic duo' isn't synonymous with keeping us on opening shifts for the rest of our college careers."

"Seriously. I nap every afternoon like a newborn. I miss having long luxurious nights of sleep."

"Well, we have all weekend."

"Most of the weekend. We are giving up our Friday night to do this," I remind him.

"Could be worse," he says.

-CARTER-

The first set of games gets started, and with each point, someone jogs over to us and we make a tally mark. It doesn't seem like a very good use of time because volleyball points add up quickly. So the runner is pretty much constantly running.

The first round ends, and we announce the winners. Jordan brings us pizza and says there're sodas in the fridge if we want them. And obviously, we want them.

"This might be the best Friday night I've had in a while," Paisley says. "Free pizza? Does it get better than that?"

"Why do we say Friday night?"

"Huh?" she asks around a mouthful of cheese.

"Like, why don't we say Friday when we mean day and Fri-night when we mean Friday night?"

"Are you stoned? That's definitely the kind of question a stoned person would ask."

"No, I'm not stoned. I'm serious. This is serious business. I think about this a lot," I say.

"There's a pretty good chance you have too much time on your hands."

"Well, I'm going to start a grassroots movement. If you want in, this is your chance."

"Do I want in on a grassroots movement to start using Mon-night, Tues-night, Wednes-night in regular conversation? That's what you're asking me."

"Yes."

"I just. I don't think so. That doesn't sound like something

217

I'm interested in. But I'll keep it in mind, in case something changes."

"You could make T-shirts for it! We could finance the campaign with T-shirt sales." I instantly regret bringing up the T-shirts, seeing as how it's my fault she no longer can sell them.

But it doesn't seem to faze her. "They could be like the days of the week underwear, but you know, even more ridiculous."

"So you're in, right?"

She's trying her best to keep herself from smiling.

"Hey, just think if you changed your mind about me, you can change your mind about anything."

"Which reminds me," she says. "I haven't wanted to be too nosy, but how did the exam go the other day?"

"Better than expected? But who knows. It seemed awfully easy."

"That's thanks to the Paisley Turner Simple Calculus Method. You're just seeing the fruits of our labor."

We make a little more small talk, and then I suck in a deep breath.

"So, in the interest of being more open about things, and since you asked me to keep you updated, my mom has a big doctor's appointment tomorrow morning. I wanted to go home for it, but Thea insisted I didn't need to. She's getting a bunch of tests and scans, and I'm really nervous."

"I can imagine," Paisley says carefully.

"I'm honestly happy to be here or else I'd just be in my room, worrying all night."

"This isn't exactly the best distraction," she says, gesturing toward the courts. "Or maybe it is. I mean, there's something sort of chaotic about four volleyball matches at once."

"Well, anyway. I guess I just wanted to get that out there."

"I could distract you."

"How?"

"I don't know. With, like, the kind of games that are usually played on long car rides. Or maybe a series of escalating dares."

He laughs. And I laugh with him.

Jordan stops by in the middle of the third round. Her game is in a time-out because one of the players took a ball to the face.

"What are you two giggling about over here?" she asks.

"Nothing much," I say.

"Dynamic duo, I tell you," Jordan says, mostly to herself as she walks away.

I can tell we're both blushing, but that's a good thing, I figure.

-PAISLEY-

Now it's my turn to confess something that I'm nervous about.

"So I talked to Henry."

"About what?" Carter asks only half paying attention to me. He's tallying up the game from court number three.

"About you. About what you told me on Halloween. About middle school."

He turns to me with a raised eyebrow. "And?"

"And he confirmed what you said. That was exactly what happened."

"Good."

I'm about to say something else when a volleyball comes flying toward our table and directly for Carter's face. I spike it out of the way.

"Oh my god," he says. "You saved my life. I saw my whole life flash before my eyes. I thought for sure I was going to die."

"I don't think volleyballs are made to kill people. You would have gotten a pretty bad bloody nose, though."

"You are totally my hero."

"I will happily accept that title."

The time seems to drag after that, even though we play round after round of I Spy. It's hard to really find new things after a while.

"I spy with my little eye, someone in a red T-shirt."

I roll my eyes. "Carter, there's a full team of people in red T-shirts. I'm wearing a red T-shirt."

"I noticed. I also noticed it has no message."

"Sometimes a T-shirt is just a T-shirt."

"I've gotten used to reading your mood via what it says on your shirt."

"Well," I say. "Today it means that sometimes a T-shirt is just a T-shirt."

-CARTER-

When the games are over, Jordan sends us home.

"You're sure you don't need help cleaning up?" Paisley asks.

"Yeah, I'm sure. I have the third-shift maintenance staff coming soon to help. We finished a little earlier than expected or else they'd already be here."

It's a few minutes past midnight when we get outside. The moon is almost full, and the air is cold enough to see our breaths.

"Feels like it could snow," Paisley says.

"It kind of does." I pull out my phone and check the temperature. "Although, according to the weather app, it's forty-two degrees outside, so definitely a little on the warm side for snow."

"When did forty-two degrees start to feel so cold?"

"Because it was seventy, like, last week."

"That would be why," Paisley agrees.

When we get to the dorm, I don't want the night to end.

"I was supposed to go meet Stef at a party at the swim house, but I just can't quite bring myself to change and head back out."

"I totally hear you. But I'm kind of awake."

She's on her phone texting Stef. When she finishes, she looks up at me.

"Want to come upstairs and watch a movie?" she asks.

"Yeah, that sounds good."

"Not even going to ask what movie? What if I force you to watch a really bad rom-com on Netflix?"

"Honestly, I like rom-coms, especially the ones on Netflix."

We take the elevator up and walk down the hall and around the bend. I'm almost nervous, not sure what "watching a movie on Netflix" means to Paisley. Maybe something could happen tonight.

But then I notice someone sitting on the floor outside her room, leaning on the door, a backpack at his feet, a textbook open on his lap.

"Henry?" Paisley asks.

He looks up.

And there he is. Henry Lai. The boy who I terrorized in middle school.

Definitely not the way I expected this evening to go.

CHAPTER EIGHTEEN

-PAISLEY-

"Henry?"

He looks up at me and his whole body radiates stress. I slide down onto the floor next to him.

"What are you doing here?" I ask.

"Uh. Well. I just needed to talk to you. Face-to-face." He looks over at Carter. Carter sticks his hand out to shake Henry's, and I feel this inexplicable softness toward him. Even softer when Henry stands to accept the handshake.

"Hey, man," Carter says. "How are you?"

"Um. Pretty good, um," Henry says, glancing between Carter and me. "I hope I'm not interrupting something."

"Nothing at all," Carter says. "We had to work late tonight so I was just escorting Paisley safely to her room."

"Barf," I say. "He was coming up here to watch a movie. But I'll see you tomorrow, Carter."

"Yeah," he says, nodding, taking the hint. "See you tomorrow."

"Hey," I say, catching his attention as he heads for the stairs. "I hope everything goes really well for your mom."

"Thanks," he says. "I'll keep you posted."

When Carter has retreated into the stairwell, I turn my full attention to Henry.

"So you didn't waste any time there, huh?" Henry asks, a grin breaking out on his face. He seems so much more relaxed all of a sudden. He sits back down next to me and starts collecting his belongings. He'd obviously been camped out in the hallway for a while.

"I mean, we really were working late. He was going to watch a movie with me. That's all."

"Oh right. 'Watching a movie,'" he says, putting air quotes around the phrase. "That's obviously some kind of euphemism, I'm sure."

I roll my eyes and give him an awkward side hug.

"I'm glad you're here. Why are you here?"

"Can we maybe go inside before I spill my soul?"

"Oh right, yeah."

I open the door. "Why didn't you text me?"

"I was going to. I figured you'd be coming home eventually and I had a lot of work to get done. I kind of lost track of time."

He sits down at my desk and looks at the pictures I have taped up above it. I take a seat on my bed and squeeze my pillow.

"It's good to know you're a little bit sentimental."

"I'm very much sentimental. And I'm happy to see you, but I'm more than a little worried that you'd show up here unannounced. It's not like you live around the block."

"Yeah, the six-hour bus and train ride here was not fun."

"So why did you come? Again, not that I'm not happy to see you, but it feels like you're dancing around something."

"Well. You know how we talked the day after Halloween?"

"Yes . . ."

"So I kind of forgot to mention something that morning. Or not forgot. I failed to mention something."

"Always so precise," I say, trying to lighten the mood.

He twists his fingers in his lap. "I had sex with my calc TA. I had sex with Jana," he says in a rush. "On Halloween. I can't believe I did that and I can't believe I'm here telling you I did that. And I'm racked with guilt about it."

I fall back on my bed and cover my face. Henry had sex. I let that sink in. Then I sit back up.

"You're judging me," he says.

"No, I'm not. I'm taking it in. That's great, Henry. As long as you think it's great. But I'm getting the feeling that you don't think it's great."

"It's fine. It's okay. I like her a lot and I wanted to do it. If that's what you're asking. I just can't believe I did that. I shouldn't have done that."

"But you did," I say gently. "I know you, Henry. If you didn't want to, you wouldn't have."

"I know. You're right. I wanted to have sex with Jana."

"Have you talked to her? Like have you and Jana discussed this?" Her name feels weird in my mouth, like it's some sacred word I shouldn't be using. I guess it's because of how Henry says it, with such reverence.

"I have."

"And are things okay?"

"Yeah, she likes me too. I told her that we shouldn't be together because she's my TA, and she said it was no big deal. That there aren't any rules about it. But what if she gets fired for fraternizing or something? Then that's all my fault."

"Well, no," I say. "That's her own fault. She's a grown-up. She can make these decisions for herself."

"Okay. Yes. But I'm still party to them."

"Listen, Henry, you're obviously a wonderful person and I'm happy that someone likes you. But you're not so wonderful that she can't contain herself. That when she's around you she just wants to rip off your clothes. You're not . . . Fabio."

"Wow, another timely and humorous pop culture reference from you," he says.

"You can be as sarcastic as you want about my timely and humorous pop culture references, but my point still stands. As long as this was consensual on both sides, there's nothing wrong with what happened."

"But it's unethical!" Henry insists.

"I know, I know, buckaroo. I know the ethics of it upsets you. But really, I don't think it's that big of a deal. Or it's only as big of a deal as you make it. If you want it to be a huge deal, that's fine. But if you want to be with her, to be with Jana, then you need to come to terms with the ethics."

He rubs his face. "You're right. I knew you'd make me feel better."

"I made you feel better? Just like that?" I ask, snapping my fingers.

"Just like that," he says.

"So you're going to leave now?"

He laughs. "Yeah, you know, I figure I'll head right back. Twenty minutes with you would be worth the twelve-hour round trip."

He stands and stretches before coming to sit next to me on my bed.

"So, let's watch whatever movie you were going to watch with Carter, and you can tell me all about how you love him."

I hit him with my pillow. "I don't love him."

"Sure, sure, whatever you say." He grabs my pillow and rolls it behind his neck, making himself comfortable.

-CARTER-

In the morning, Ray and I are both home for once. When I wake up, he's standing in the middle of our room wearing nothing but a towel and staring wide-eyed at his phone.

I check the time. It's only nine. I'm not sure how I'm going to make it until this afternoon when I'll hopefully hear about how my mom's doctor's appointment went.

"Hey, you okay?" I ask, sitting up.

"What are you up to today?" he asks, still not looking at me.

"Nothing. I don't have work or anything." I wouldn't have minded spending the day with Paisley, but that was likely a pipe dream even before Henry showed up. "Why, what's up?"

He hands me his phone and moves over to his closet to pull on a pair of shorts.

"What am I looking at?"

"A group text about the trivia team. One of the guys got mono and he can't compete today. We really need a stand-in or else we'll have to forfeit."

"I thought you had a ton of alternates or whatever."

He pulls a T-shirt over his head. "We did. But I guess they've all been making out with each other because they all have mono too. And one of them has to go to a wedding."

"Wow. What the hell kind of parties are you guys having? Maybe I don't want to help you out if all it's going to get me is mono."

"Please, man, I'm begging you here. For some reason, there's no one else available this weekend on short notice. We need a body."

In the spirit of roommate bonding, I say, "Sure. I can be a body. It'll be a good distraction from waiting around to hear about my mom's test results."

"Oh man, that's today?" Ray asks, stopping in the middle of whirling around the room and getting ready.

"Yeah. This is great, though. This is exactly the diversion I need."

"Good. Do you own a tie?"

"Yes."

"Do you have said tie with you?"

"Yes."

After that, it's quick work getting dressed, meeting the rest of the team at the dining hall for breakfast, and then getting on the bus.

"I had no idea there were girls on this team," I say to Ray as we take our seats.

"Of course there are girls," he says, giving me a weird look.

"You just never mention them."

"Weird," he says. "I'll have to do better."

The bus ride is about an hour, so I scroll through my phone, playing whatever games don't waste data, and soon enough we're at the tournament.

It's the kind of day that flies by. We move from one round to the next, with barely five minutes to get from one room to another.

I have trouble keeping up at first, and I definitely make a couple of mistakes, but in the end, I get more questions right than I get wrong, so I'd call that a win. Especially since I don't embarrass myself too much in the process.

We place third in our division, which means the team will be going on to the next round.

Ray high-fives me. "What do you say? You want to join?"

"Hell, yeah," I say. "If you guys want me."

"Dude, mono can last a long time. We need to make sure you're prepped and ready for regionals the first weekend of December."

I nod. "Sounds good to me."

When I finally check my phone, I realize I hadn't

thought once about my mom all day. We had to hand our phones in before the first round and didn't even get them back during lunch. I texted Thea this morning to let her know I wouldn't be available but that she should text me no matter what the news was.

And then I see the words "No disease detected."

I scroll through her texts and reread.

"What's up with your mom?" Ray asks, reading over my shoulder. I lean so he can read along with me.

When I don't say anything, Ray keeps reading. "All the tests showed normal organ function and no disease detected."

I'm glad he's reading because my eyes are blurring with tears. I knew I was worried about this, but it's like I couldn't acknowledge how worried I was until right this second. And now, everything is going to be fine.

Ray gives me a sort of awkward side bro hug, but I appreciate it.

This is officially the best day I've had in a long, long time.

-PAISLEY-

I feel bad that Henry slept on the floor last night even though Stef never came home. I've texted her a couple of times today, but apparently she was just "out." Which seems weird to me and like she's pissed off, but I have Henry to deal with.

We went to the dining hall for breakfast and I made him eat waffles. Then we hung out in the sunshine for a while.

And I swear with each passing hour, he became more and more comfortable with the idea of what he did. Like he had been in denial up to that point. I swear I should write a guidebook about the care and keeping of your introverted best friend.

When we get back to the room that afternoon, Stef has obviously been there but is no longer around.

"Are you feeling better?" I ask Henry.

He's sitting at my desk, preparing to do work. Which seems like a bit much to me on a Saturday afternoon, but he promised that once he did a little bit more homework that we could have a Marvel movie marathon, starting with *Captain America: Civil War.*

"Yeah, I think I just needed some distance," he says.

"So you're going to talk to her? Be normal about things? Maybe not run away next time?"

His cheeks redden. "Yeah. Man, I hope there's a next time." He drums his pencil on his book and gets to work.

I text Stef again, trying to get a gauge on her mood.

Paisley: So, what are you up to? Henry and I are going to have a movie marathon tonight if you want to join in.

Stef: Um. Maybe. I've been hanging out with Melissa.

Paisley: Is that where you were last night?!?!

Stef: Well, Melissa's apartment, with her and her roommates. Not actually WITH her.

Paisley: Still good. Is she still with that guy?

Stef: Yeah. ☹

Paisley: Too bad.

Stef: So did you know Henry was coming?

Paisley: Nope. He showed up on our doorstep like a sad puppy. He's having an emotional/romantical crisis.

Stef: Oh. Poor guy. Well. I probably will come back soon. I stopped by earlier to shower, but now I'm exhausted.

Paisley: Yeah, I noticed you'd been here. What have you been up to?

Stef: Swim practice, then the mall. Nothing too interesting.

Paisley: All right. Well, hopefully you'll be home just in time to watch Bucky and his beautiful hair.

Stef: Ugh. He has such amazing hair.

I look over at Henry and realize that his hour of work is almost up. At that moment, he closes his textbook and looks over at me.

"You pop the popcorn and I'll go get us sodas?" he asks.

"Works for me," I say.

He steps out of the room.

-CARTER-

I've been pacing in the hallway in front of Paisley's room for ten minutes. It was so quiet in there, I almost wasn't sure if she was home. And maybe if she was home, she was napping. And I would hate to wake a sleeping Paisley.

But then the door swings open and Henry appears. So the decision is made for me.

"Hey," he says.

"Hey. I need to apologize to you."

"Has Paisley blackmailed you into this?"

I chuckle. "It's not Paisley. I mean. She's part of it. But this isn't about her. This is something I need to do. I need to make things okay between us. If I can't take back everything I did, I at least want to make things okay."

"Okaaay," he says, sticking his hands in his pockets. "I mean. It's history, you know? You were dealing with some shit."

"Yeah, things sucked pretty hard back then," I agree.

"Yeah, I figured if someone was crying every day in the bathroom in middle school, it must have been pretty shitty."

"How astute of you."

"You're not actually the first person to ever call me astute."

"I bet," I say.

"Anything else?" he asks.

"So you accept my apology? I feel like I'm in a twelve-step program. Like I can't move on to the next step without your okay. I don't even know what the next step is." I'm babbling. I know I'm babbling. But that doesn't mean I can stop myself. I cross my arms in front of me and then uncross them.

"Yes. Of course I accept your apology. I don't tend to hold grudges."

"Unlike Paisley."

"Well, Paisley is something else. She's special."

"She is," I agree.

He sighs and I know he wants nothing more than to move past this and walk away from me.

Instead he says, "I'm not gonna do that thing. That macho thing where I tell you that if you hurt her, I'll hurt you. Because she doesn't need me to do that. If you hurt her, she'll hurt you."

"I do not doubt that for a second."

"But, like. Good luck with her. I don't mean that sarcastically. I just know you're gonna need it."

I laugh.

"I hope you figure out whatever it is you need to figure out. Both of you. Because there's obviously something happening. I mean, the fact that both of you have now talked to me about this seems statistically significant if nothing else."

"If nothing else," I agree. "Thanks, Henry."

Paisley and I are, if nothing else, statistically significant.

"You want to come in?" Henry asks.

"Nah," I say, shaking my head. "You guys have fun."

"All right," he says, turning toward the vending machines.

"Tell Paisley I'll see her tomorrow."

"Will do." Then he does this little salute and heads down the hall.

CHAPTER NINETEEN

-PAISLEY-

"Who were you talking to outside?" I ask when Henry comes back into the room.

"Carter," he says simply, placing our bottles of soda on my desk and not looking at me.

"Carter was in the hallway?"

"Yeah."

"Did you invite him in?"

"He seemed to want to talk to me."

"Are you going to give me any further information?"

Henry looks over at me and considers the question. "No."

"Rude."

He shrugs.

Stef comes in a few minutes later, and we settle in to watch *Captain America: Civil War*. But it's hard to concentrate. I want to ask Henry a million questions.

We fall asleep halfway through *Ant-Man* and in the

morning we head out for breakfast. I keep my eyes peeled for Carter, but he's nowhere around. As soon as we're done eating, it'll be time to bring Henry to the train station. Where unfortunately, he'll have to take the train to the bus, just to get back to Penn State.

But on our way out of the dining hall, we run into Carter and Ray.

Finally.

"Hey, you know, I don't have your phone number," Carter says by way of greeting.

"You don't have my phone number," I repeat, like he said this sentence in a language I don't quite understand. And maybe it is a language I don't quite understand.

"Yeah, you know. Like for the texting."

"Are you a good texter?" I ask.

"Fair to middling," he says.

"That doesn't really sound worth my while," I tell him with a quirk of my eyebrow.

My god, the flirting. We are world-champion flirters, I think. Unless we're both really bad flirters and it feels so right because we're on the same level. There's a lot to unpack there.

"I'll get better. You could train me," he insists.

"I could train you? Like a parrot."

"Exactly. I bet if given the opportunity, parrots would be excellent texters."

"This conversation has gotten completely out of hand," Stef says. "And if we don't leave now, Henry is going to be stranded here."

I nod. "Give me your phone," I say to Carter.

I type in my number and hand it back to him. "Text me so I have yours."

Henry, Stef, and I turn toward the direction of town and Carter continues on to the dining hall.

"Talk to you tomorrow," Carter calls over his shoulder.

"Yeah, tomorrow," I say.

"That was . . . interesting," Henry says as we head off campus.

"If by interesting you mean awkward as hell," Steph says.

"Well, you're both weirdos, so that helps," Henry says.

"Thanks," I say.

But even after saying goodbye to Henry, something still feels off. I end up texting him during his bus ride.

> **Paisley:** So I think I can go for it with Carter now, right?
>
> **Henry:** I don't know why you think you need my permission. Haven't we been over this? Like fourteen times?
>
> **Paisley:** I need to know. I can tell something is brewing and I need reassurance from you.
>
> **Henry:** Listen, I barely care about this. I only care about it as much as I do because it involves you and I'd like you to be happy. But I could give a shit about you being happy with Carter.

Paisley: Explain. Because that sounds bad.

Henry: It doesn't matter who you're with as long as you're happy. I don't care if it's with Carter.

Paisley: Okay. That's what I thought you meant. But I have a hard time believing that you'd be okay with it.

Henry: Why?

Paisley: I don't know. Honestly.

Henry: Is it because you think I'm stubborn? Or because I don't get over things? Or because I don't understand my own feelings? Or because you think I'm lying to you to protect your feelings?

Paisley: No to all of that. Minus the stubborn thing. You can be stubborn but I don't think you're being stubborn about this. I don't understand what exactly you're being about this. I can't get a good read on you.

Henry: Here's the thing, Paisley. Likely,

someday, one of us might have a boyfriend
or a girlfriend that comes between us.

Paisley: I'm never going to let that
happen.

Henry: Just stop for a second. Let me
finish. I'm not saying it's going to happen. I'm saying that it might happen.
That it could happen.

Paisley: Well, if that happens, then
we're not as good of friends as I thought
we were.

Henry: PAISLEY. PLEASE. I just want to
make a point.

Paisley: I don't like this hypothetical
and I will not entertain it.

Henry: BUT IT COULD HAPPEN.

Paisley: NO. NEVER. I WILL NOT ALLOW IT.

Henry: Are you done now? Are you ready
to listen?

Paisley: Okay. Fine. I'll stop now.

Henry: I'm just saying that I don't think the person that will come between us is Carter Schmitt. Like, I don't think he has that kind of force in our lives. I don't believe it for a second. Just do it, Paisley. Rip off the Band-Aid. All this hemming and hawing about what it will do to our relationship is an excuse at this point. Because it's not about Carter or me or anyone else. It's about you.

Paisley: Those are a lot of words, Henry.

Henry: I mean every one of them.

Paisley: You can't see me nodding, but I am.

Henry: Just do it, Paisley. Make your move.

Paisley: What if he's not worth it?

Henry: There's only one way to find out.

Paisley: I hate it when you're right.

Henry: You must hate me a majority of the time.

Paisley: Only when you're also smug about being right.

Henry: So, quite often.

Paisley: Maybe you feel like telling me about what you and Carter talked about in the hallway last night?

Henry: Nah.

Paisley: Dammit, Henry.

-CARTER-

I had really hoped to hear from Paisley last night, but nothing. No word from her. I know the ball is in my court and all that, but I feel like I could foul out of the game if I'm not careful.

I can't stop thinking about her T-shirt from a few months ago that said "Let the games begin."

Also, I need to stop playing basketball with Ray because I only think in sports metaphors for days after and wind up annoying myself.

I solemnly swear that if I don't hear from her tonight, that I'll text her tomorrow. Even though we have three classes together tomorrow. And even though what I really want to do is take her on a date and I don't know how to accomplish that.

In the morning, I go through the motions of opening the gym. I'm on this morning with Jordan, which is fine, but I wish it were Paisley. We need to talk. And we get our best talking done early in the morning. Or maybe not our "best" talking, but definitely our most real talking. All bets are off when we're talking before dawn.

When the gym opens at six thirty, there's the usual small rush of people who wander in to use the machines or the weights or the pool on their way to work.

Instead of doing homework, I decide to jot down ideas for dates. I start the list with dinner, movie, the generic stuff. I want to think of something better. Something exciting. Easier said than done.

But then, as if I summoned her with my thoughts, she's standing in front of me, holding out a cup of coffee.

"Bless you," I say.

"I didn't sneeze," she says.

I roll my eyes.

"Jokes are really hard to make this early in the morning," she says.

"How come you're not on the schedule?" I ask, taking the paper cup from her. She obviously trekked to the student center for this, going that extra mile.

"I'm honestly not sure." She peers at the schedule behind the desk. "I'm on for the rest of the week at six, though."

"Well, at least I'll be here with you tomorrow, but I have off the rest of the week after that."

"Lucky you," she says. "Who's on with you this morning?"

"Jordan," I say.

She slides into the seat next to me. Jordan's office door is closed at the moment, and the light next to her extension is on. We have a few minutes at least.

"Who does she even talk to on the phone at seven o'clock in the morning?" I ask.

"Her mom. Her priest. Her psychic," Paisley says.

I snort into my coffee.

"First of all, how's your mom?"

I grin. "She's good. All the tests came back negative, or positive, or however we wanted them to come back. All good news."

"That's awesome," she says.

We nod at each other.

"So, what do you say?" she asks.

"About what?" I feel like I missed something, like I took a micro-nap and missed the subject change.

"Oh, come on," she says, spinning in the chair. "Are you really going to make me spell it out for you?'

"It's so early in the morning the sun is barely awake, and you expect me to know what you're talking about? I can't play games this early."

"You're doing a good job of pretending to be obtuse."

She puts the toe of her sneaker down as a brake to stop spinning and looks at me.

I smirk.

She smirks right back.

She might have the best smirk that I have ever seen. She probably practices it in the mirror. That seems like something Paisley would do, just to get the right vibe going. To put exactly what she wants out in the world.

"What do you think?" I ask.

"About you being obtuse? It's annoying sometimes. Sometimes it's cute, kind of like a puppy."

"I was once likened to a golden retriever puppy by my history teacher in ninth grade. I could never quite shake the idea. I think it's pretty apt."

"But I don't know what to think. In general," she says, spinning again.

"Do you think you want to, I don't know, go on a date with me or something?"

She spins toward me and smirks again. This is the smirkiest conversation I have ever had. Like, what are we both so smirky about?

She moves her chair closer to mine, so that our knees touch. The light is still on at Jordan's extension, and I feel like something is about the happen.

She puts her hands on the arms of my chair and looks me full in the face. It's a lot of eye contact for so early. And I have coffee breath.

But she knows that. She's the one who brought me the coffee.

"Why are we playing eye contact chicken while I have coffee breath?" I ask.

This time I get a genuine smile, nothing like a smirk. A smile so bold and bright it could shame the sun. I've never seen an expression like that on Paisley's face before. She always seems like so many shades of cool, and aloof, and above it all.

But right now she isn't.

Right now, she's here with me. Being not cool, and not aloof, and not above it all.

"I don't know," she says. I know she's about to say more. I know something is supposed to happen. But then Jordan's extension goes dark and Paisley notices.

"That's my cue to leave, but I'll see you later, right?"

I nod and she's gone, but I know something is finally happening.

-PAISLEY-

It's Friday night, and Ray and Carter are having everyone over to play video games. And by everyone, I mean a couple of guys from the trivia team and me. I asked Stef if she wanted to come along, but remarkably she did not think this sounded like a great Friday night.

Someone brought some beer but I'm staying away from the stuff. It makes me gassy. I don't need to be gassy. I just want to sit next to Carter and hang out and make jokes. When did I become this person?

I go out to use the restroom, but when I get back, Carter is standing in the hallway, leaning against the wall.

"I thought maybe we could take a walk or something."

"Oh yeah?"

"Yeah, the guys decided to have a fart contest, and now it smells so bad in there. I don't want you to have to deal with that."

"My poor cell phone," I say, holding out my hand as if I could reach through the wall for it.

"I'll save it," he says. Before I can stop him, he's pulled his T-shirt up over his nose and slid back inside.

When he comes out with my phone, I clasp my hands together and say, "My hero."

"I do what I can, ma'am," he says in a deep voice.

He runs a hand through his hair, making it stand on end. I want to put my hands in his hair.

"So, a walk?" he says.

It's raining and cold out. I don't want to take a walk. But there's something I really want to do, and I don't know how to get from here, standing next to each other, to there. *There* being kissing.

"I think I'll let you make out with me again." I decide to go with the direct approach.

"You'll let me?"

"Maybe," I say.

"So kind. So generous."

I stand on my tiptoes to reach his mouth and it's immediately perfect. It's everything I dreamed of since that night in the basement when we first made out. I let my fingers dance along the hairline at the back of his neck, and his arm comes around my waist. I forgot just how strong he feels. I made myself forget. I didn't want to think about it, about him, about his lips.

We stay in the hallway for a long time. I'm not even sure how long. Not really. I think a few people pass us, at least one because we get a wolf whistle.

By that point, I'm basically trying to become one with Carter, pushing him up against the wall, wanting to get as close to him as possible. I can't help it.

Apparently, a sexual animal has lived inside of me all this time. It only took Carter to bring it out.

A head peeks out of the room.

Someone clears their throat.

"Oh, there you are," Ray says. "So this is a thing now, huh?"

Ray seems only a little surprised, unless he's really good at keeping a poker face.

"Yup," Carter says, his voice breathy but his lips never leave mine.

"Are you guys ever coming back in?" Ray asks. "Or do you live in this hallway now?"

"Live in the hallway," Carter says without stopping kissing.

"Do you two hallway dwellers want anything from the pizza place?"

I pull away from Carter's lips and I swear I hear a small *pop*.

I feel much colder immediately.

"Yes. I want cheese fries," I say. Cheese fries and kissing Carter, I'm not sure I could ever imagine a better night.

"I'll have a slice of whatever you're getting," Carter says.

"All right. Cool."

He closes the door. We hear him say to the room, "They're out there making out. But they do have requests."

I nuzzle my nose into Carter's chin, inhaling, and happy to find that he doesn't smell like beer tonight.

"You smell really amazing."

"I have no idea why. I literally use generic bodywash."

"Well, it's good-smelling generic bodywash," I say.

"We might as well keep making out until the food comes, right?" he asks.

"Of course."

So we get back to it.

Except that doesn't last long. When Ray goes to get the pizza, he comes back and says, "Paisley, I think your room-mate is crying in the lobby."

"What? Why?"

Ray shrugs.

"Um, I better go check what that's about," I say. Carter tries to follow me but I stop him. "I think it's best if I go alone. I'll come back later."

When I get to the lobby, she spots me immediately. She's obviously worked up.

"Where were you?" she asks. I've never seen her so shaken. "I texted you and called you like eighty times."

"I wasn't paying attention to my phone. I was with Carter. I told you where I was going."

"And I told you that I was going down the hall and not to lock the door."

"And I thought you said to lock the door because you were going out."

"I didn't even have shoes on, Paisley!" She kicks her foot up to demonstrate the fact that she's only wearing socks.

"I'm sorry. I wasn't paying very good attention. Why didn't you come and get me?"

She ignores my question in favor of getting more pissed off. "I really needed to get a good night's sleep tonight because we have an exhibition meet and I have to be up at five."

"I'm sorry," I tell her. "I'm sorry I missed your calls and texts. Where's Kenny? Couldn't he unlock the door?"

"He's not around and you know there's a fee. And I don't have money to pay a fee."

"I thought it was like ten bucks?" I say.

"I heard it was more like a hundred," Stef says, sniffling. "And I don't have a hundred dollars right now."

I rub her back. "I'm really sorry. It's only ten thirty. You can still get some sleep."

I lead Stef to our room.

"I really am sorry," I say.

"You're just so wrapped up in everything that's going on with Carter that you don't even care about anything else."

I want to argue with her, but I know that she's fighting with me for the sake of fighting with me.

"I'm sorry," I repeat for the third time. "I didn't mean to lock you out."

"Sure, whatever," she says. She grabs her stuff and goes into the bathroom to shower.

Carter texts me to say that my food is waiting for me. He adds:

Carter: You could come sleep down here.

Paisley: Thanks for the offer, but I might as well face the music up here.

Maybe I'll come down after she's gone to
bed.

Carter: All right, it's up to you.

Paisley: Keep my cheese fries warm.

He shoots back a bunch of thumbs-up emojis.

But Stef doesn't say another word to me when she gets out of the shower. She turns out the lights and throws herself under the covers.

I take that as my cue to go back down to Carter. It's not like I need to be up at five in the morning for once. I might as well continue my evening.

"Good luck tomorrow," I say.

"Thank you," she mumbles.

And with that I close the door behind me.

CHAPTER TWENTY

-CARTER-

My phone rings early Sunday morning, and I curse myself for not putting it on "do not disturb." Ray spent the night at his brother's so at least the ringing didn't wake him up too.

When I answer, Thea starts talking without preamble.

"I have to tell you something, but you're not going to like it." I'm so tired it takes me a minute to catch up. Paisley was over until three in the morning. I'm not entirely sure why she even bothered to go back to her room.

"I have something to tell you that you won't like either. But tell me yours first."

"Dad wants to see you," she says.

"How nice. Too bad that I'm very busy avoiding him."

"Come on, Carter."

"Come on where?" I roll over and hide my face in my pillow.

"Don't be obtuse. I'm just saying."

"Whatever," I mumble into my pillow, letting my eyes close. I like it when Paisley calls me obtuse but not when Thea does. I consider hanging up on her, but she'll just call me back. And if I don't answer, I can totally imagine her driving down here to bother me in person.

"I can't hear you, Carter."

"I don't have to see him if I don't want to see him," I say, flipping back over onto my side and sitting up.

"It's been years. Literally years since you saw him."

"I'm going to amend that statement. It's been literally years since *he* saw *me*."

"Will you at least consider it?"

"Thea, I don't need to consider it. My answer is no."

"What if I told you Mom wanted you to see him?"

"I would say why didn't he show up sooner, like in the spring, when she was diagnosed. I'm so tired of his excuses."

"Is he a mind reader?" She huffs out a breath. "I didn't tell him. I'm assuming you didn't tell him she was sick. I know Mom didn't. He wants to be around now. And he's coming to see his parents."

"Oh, those people. The ones who totally stopped calling after our parents got divorced. Yeah, they don't mean anything to me."

"Mom asked them to stop calling. She didn't want to hear from them. She made that decision. Dad's allowed to see his family. And I'm allowed to see Dad if I want. And to talk to him."

"I never said you couldn't. I said that I don't want to." Why is this so hard for her to understand? I could ask her that, but I also just want this conversation to be over.

"Just think about it? Don't make any rash decisions?" she says, the pleading in her voice almost more than I can take.

"I don't think my feelings will change."

"All right. Maybe you could pretend. For me."

"Fine. I'll pretend. For you."

"That's a good boy."

"I'm rolling my eyes so hard right now," I say. "You can't see it. But I am."

She laughs. "So what did you want to tell me that I don't want to hear?"

I was going to tell her that things with Paisley are progressing. But I don't feel like fighting with her anymore. "I forgot," I lie. "I think I was dreaming."

-PAISLEY-

Carter is working Monday morning and I'm not. I decide to go see him. Even though I literally saw him less than twelve hours ago.

We kind of, sort of, spent the entire weekend making out. Luckily Stef was away at her swim meet all day Saturday and Ray spent Saturday night at his brother's. That definitely helped.

"Hey," Carter says when I walk into the fitness center.

I lean over the desk and peck him on the lips. "Who are you on with this morning?"

"Dara," he says, and then in an abrupt subject change, he continues on. "We should go on a date."

"On a what?" I ask.

"You know, a date. Make an honest man out of me and all that."

"How is this my problem? I'm happy to just make out with you in and around the dorm."

He gestures for me to come around the side of the desk and pats his lap.

"Are you serious?" I ask.

He nods and waggles his eyebrows so I settle on his knees. I worry that this is the chair that I yanked the screw out of back when I hated Carter. What if it's no longer structurally sound?

"I don't know. What kind of date would we even go on?" I ask, putting my arms around his neck and trying to get comfortable.

"I don't know. That's why you're in charge of it. You're far more creative than I am. You and your T-shirts and your imagination."

"I don't have that good of an imagination."

"You and your T-shirts and your corny puns."

"I have the best puns," I say.

"We don't have to, like, define the relationship," he says. "But it might be nice to go somewhere besides your room, my room, work, and class."

"And the dining hall. We go to the dining hall together."

"And the dining hall," he says.

"This is going to take some thinking. I'm going to have to scramble the brain trust and see what they come up with. Going on a date that doesn't cost a lot of money and is better than going to the dining hall and then coming back to my room to make out is going to be tough to come by."

"That's why I truly think you're up for the challenge," he says.

"When do you want to go on this date?"

He shrugs.

"Maybe I'll simplify things and make you take me out while we're home for Thanksgiving in a mere forty-eight hours from now."

"That seems like cheating," he says.

"You know you could help instead of complain," I say.

"But isn't it more fun this way?"

"More fun for who?" I asked.

"More fun for whom," he corrects.

"Is it really whom? Are you making that up? Is it ever whom?"

"It is."

I twirl a pen in my fingers, and it flies out of my hand and rolls under the desk. I slide off Carter's lap to retrieve it.

"Ugh. I can't reach," I say.

"Let me help you." He joins me under the desk.

My cardigan snags on something, so I pull it off and toss it away.

Carter grins. "Well, that was sexy."

"Was it?" I ask, dubious.

He leans over to kiss me. I am totally weak when it comes to Carter kisses. So even though I know we could get in trouble, I almost lean in too.

But then my conscience gets the better of me.

"We really shouldn't do that here," I say.

"It's not like anyone can see us," he insists, even though our legs are pretty obviously sticking out from under the desk. "It's been so quiet all morning," he continues, his voice just a little whiny. Even one little bit whinier and I would have said no. But once again, I find myself completely weak to the idea of making out with him.

I'm about to kiss him and that's when I hear it.

The click of fancy dress shoes on the tiled floor.

"I know there are two people under the desk in various states of undress. This is inappropriate, as per the memo that was posted earlier this semester. I will see you in my office as soon as you're decent and off the clock."

The footsteps recede.

"Shit," Carter says.

"Guess we're both out of jobs," I say, trying to hold in a laugh. Why is my first instinct to laugh? Is that what shock does to a person?

We slide out from under the desk and the full force of the situation hits me.

I put my hand on my forehead. "Oh my god, we're going to lose our jobs."

"I'll go," Carter says. "I'll take the hit. You're not even on the clock. I don't think he saw you. And I already have two strikes anyway."

"We weren't making out!" I say. "We hadn't even kissed yet."

"I know, but he doesn't know that. I'm not sure he'd

accept an excuse like that. And we were about to. The only reason we didn't is because he interrupted." He sets his shoulders straight and takes a deep breath. "It's fine. I wasn't long for this world. I'm sure another strike would have come up sooner or later."

"But you need the money," I say.

"So do you," he says. "Especially since it was my fault that you had to fold your online T-shirt empire."

"I was the T-shirt mogul of Robinson Hall for a brief moment there."

"Have I apologized for that?" he asks, squinting at me.

"Once or twice," I say, sliding away from him.

"At least I was smart enough to get a scholarship," he says.

I laugh. "Thanks for making jokes at a time like this."

-CARTER-

Paisley leaves a few minutes later and then my shift is over. It's time to face the music. I walk as slowly as possible up to the manager's office on the third floor. I knock on the door. The room is intimidating, so different from the rest of the building.

I can't help but notice that there's a window behind his desk that looks directly down to the reception area. So he could see us. He saw what was happening from his office. And he could definitely see our legs and Paisley's discarded sweater.

It all makes sense now, how he would have been walking by at just the right moment. Or the wrong moment, really.

I'm not shocked when he fires me. I have no interest in excuses or explaining myself.

I'm probably going to get an ulcer worrying about how and where I'll make up that money, but I'm not going to tell him that. There are plenty of jobs on and around campus. Not many where I'll be able to get homework done while working, but let's be real, I wasn't getting that much homework done between six and nine in the morning anyway.

"Where's the girl you were with?"

"She doesn't work here. So I'm the only person who needs to be punished."

He doesn't seem pleased with that answer, but there's not much he can do. Something tells me this guy doesn't know how to use the security cameras.

I leave and move on with my day. Or at least I try to.

I don't want to dwell on this. There's almost nothing I can do about it. I didn't mean for it to happen, but it did. And I wasn't lying to Paisley; I likely wasn't going to be able to keep that job forever anyway. Having two strikes already didn't exactly give me job security.

I'll find something else, somewhere else.

Later on, I'm in Paisley's room. It feels so much better to be with Paisley than to not be with Paisley.

We're currently working on calc homework. It's my last class tomorrow before I leave for Thanksgiving break. I really need to keep my scholarship more than ever and the only way to do that is to do really, really well in my classes.

"You were amazingly cool about getting fired today," Paisley says. "I honestly can't believe you would do that."

"It's not great, but it's okay," I tell her, being as honest as possible.

I glance at my phone and sigh. Another day, another text from Thea about our dad.

"What's up?" Paisley asks.

I shake my head. "Thea's been texting me about our dad. I don't really want to get into it."

"Right. Dad stuff. I don't have one of those. So I don't have any advice or anything, but you know, I'm here if you need someone to listen."

"Thanks," I say. I want to ask about her dad, but I don't want to have to answer the same question.

"For the record," she says, like she's reading my mind, "my dad left before I was born. My mom got pregnant when she was nineteen. But it's okay, we've always had this *Gilmore Girls* thing going on that I liked."

I grin. "You would like that."

My phone buzzes again and I shove it into my bag. I roll my neck and try to relax. I don't want to end up snapping at Paisley and causing a fight, just because my dad wants to see me.

"Maybe you would feel more relaxed if we make out for a little while," she says.

I grin over at her. "Yeah?"

"Yeah."

"Meet me at the bed in three seconds," I say.

I lie down and scoot over to the wall, making room next

to me for Paisley. We can barely keep our hands off each other. Things get heated pretty fast and I'm glad the door is not only closed but also locked.

"Should we do more?" I ask. I don't really know how to say this. I'm really not very suave about this stuff. "Like, go further?"

"Maybe? I don't have a condom," she says.

"I didn't really mean right now. But yeah, I don't have one either. I have some in my room." The thrill of the idea sends a shiver through me.

"We could," she says, her voice a little nervous.

"Have you ever done it?" I ask. "Is that okay to ask?"

"Yeah, that's fine to ask." She pauses. "See, the thing is. This is kind of awkward, but you're the first person I ever kissed." She winces away from me a little and I miss her even though she's still right here. I pull her closer, trying to show her that it's not a big deal.

But I'm not sure how to respond.

"Pathetic, right?" she says with a nervous laugh.

"Nah. I only had one real girlfriend. We didn't have sex. We got to third base."

She looks at me and I can tell she's already more relaxed. "When do you think people stop talking about bases? Do adults talk in bases? Can you get to third base with your husband?"

"I don't know. I hope so. Third base is a fun base."

She laughs and the tension between us dissolves along with her nerves.

"Well, what now?" she asks. "Stef is gone for the rest of

the afternoon. She has a marathon swim practice or something. She won't be home until five or six."

"We could watch TV for a while," I say, needing to calm down a little. The mere idea of sex was almost too much to handle at the moment. "Or we could nap it out."

So we do.

We nap it out good and hard.

We sleep like we're hibernating. I hear nothing, I feel nothing, and I dream nothing.

Not until the door opens and light pours in. It could be hours or even days later and I would have no idea.

I squint into the brightness.

Stef is standing there.

So I guess it actually is much, much later.

"Hey," Paisley says, sitting up, rubbing her eyes. I'm really glad she put her shirt back on. The whole situation feels awfully vulnerable without there being exposed underwear involved.

"You guys are getting cozy," Stef says, flicking the overhead light on and dropping her bag by her bed. All my stuff is out on her desk. This is the opposite of what Paisley and I wanted to happen.

And then I realize that my jeans are on the ground.

So there is going to be some exposed underwear.

"I should go," I say, leaning over Paisley and indelicately scooping my pants up off the carpet. I swear I just about throw out my back trying to reach them.

"Yeah, we were done here," Paisley says.

"I'm sorry my stuff is over here," I say after pulling

my pants on. I leap across the room, grabbing for my calc book. "We were studying and then, you know, needed a nap."

"Is that what the kids are calling it these days?" Stef asks.

"Um, yeah, sure," I say.

After I shove everything in my bag, I kiss Paisley's temple. "Text if you want to go to dinner. I'll probably go in an hour or so."

"Sure," she says.

And then I wave to Stef and leave.

Talk about tension, I think, as I close their door behind me. And not the sexy kind.

-PAISLEY-

I end up going to the dining hall with Stef, trying my best to placate her and show her that she still matters to me.

"I really meant for him to be gone and the room to be picked up before you got back. But we fell asleep," I explain on our walk to the dining hall.

"It's cool. You don't have to, like, hide your relationship from me. I'm not some kind of shrew. I'd just like to be able to come into my room without worrying whether you and Carter are naked."

"I understand. We'll do better," I promise. And we will. I know we can. This was a fluke.

"It's not, like, this big deal," she insists. "I guess I just wanted to say something before it became a big deal and he was, like, moving in with us."

"I get it. I get what you're saying. And I promise he won't move in with us."

"Good," she says.

But there's still a simmering sort of tension between us that I don't know how to shake. I smile tight-lipped and try not to worry.

CHAPTER TWENTY-ONE

-CARTER-

It's officially Thanksgiving weekend. At least it is for me.

Paisley had to work this morning but I don't have such issues these days. I took the train home last night and I've spent pretty much the whole day doing nothing. Paisley and I made plans to meet at the mall later on for cheap food and a movie, but I still have a couple hours until I need to get ready.

I'm watching my thirteenth episode of *Family Feud*, thanks to a marathon on the Game Show Network, when the doorbell rings. My sister is at work and my mom is actually out grocery shopping for tomorrow. Her doctor only okayed her to drive last week, which means I probably should have gone with her, but she insisted on going alone. Even though it's the day before Thanksgiving.

Thea and my mom aren't living in a very big house, a little ranch with three bedrooms and one bathroom, but it's got a front door with lots of windows in it.

I wish that door were completely solid because then I wouldn't be able to see my father standing on the other side, peering in, waving at me like he's thrilled to see me.

I debate turning on my heel and walking away, hiding in the unfinished basement for the rest of my life.

Instead, I have no choice but to open the door.

He grins at me like this is a completely normal Wednesday.

"Hey there, buddy," he says. "Long time no see."

He hugs me, but I don't hug back. I don't have it in me. I used to have it in me. My dad used to be one of my favorite people in the world. I just don't know how to look at him anymore. Which is why I've spent the past five years avoiding him. It's not like he's ever really reached out either.

"Is there something you need from me?" I ask, my voice cold. I don't want to let him into the house. It's this barrier that I want to keep up. My safe space.

"Can we talk?" he asks.

I rub my jaw. "I'm not sure there's much to say."

"Aren't you happy to see me at all?"

"No, I'm really not. You can't just show up here."

"I didn't just 'show up here,'" he says, putting air quotes around the last part. "Thea invited me. I talked to her last night. She said you'd be home today. I'd love to see your mother too. I haven't seen her in a week but I hear she's on the upswing."

He doesn't deserve to see my mother and I'm so happy she's not home right now. But if I'm going to shield her from him, that means I need to get out of the house.

"I haven't eaten yet. We could go do that," I say. "Give

me a second." I close and lock the door behind me even as he moves to come inside. I run to my room and change into yesterday's jeans and throw on a hoodie.

I write a note on the back of an envelope. I need to be vague or lie, and somehow I end up doing both. "Out for a run, be back later." I don't think I've ever gone for a run in my whole life, but hopefully my mom will think I've turned over a new leaf.

We drive in silence for about ten minutes to a diner in the next town.

We sit and order, and he looks at me over the rim of his coffee mug.

"I want to apologize," he says.

"So apologize to Mom," I say.

"You don't think I have a million times?"

"I don't know what you have or haven't done."

"I've seen Thea, but you've staunchly refused to see me. You don't think that's been hard for me?"

"Obviously Thea doesn't feel abandoned."

"You feel abandoned?" He sips his coffee. "Is this about the aquarium?"

I roll my eyes. He was supposed to take me to the aquarium for my twelfth birthday. I really wanted to be a marine biologist back then. He said he had a friend who worked there who could give us a backstage tour. And then he just never picked me up.

The waitress delivers our food. I ordered French toast, because it's the only breakfast food that isn't great at the dining hall and I'm not sure why.

"This isn't about the aquarium," I say while pouring syrup over my plate.

"Then what is it about?"

"What do you think?" I say after my first bite. "I didn't understand what was going on. So I was confused. Nobody wanted to tell me anything. And Thea had just left for college and Grandma died. There was too much to deal with. Too much going on. Too much to process."

"I just want to tell you—"

"I don't want to hear it," I say, stabbing at my next piece of French toast. "I have no interest in your excuses."

"Why did you come if you don't want to listen?"

I look up at him, hopeful that my annoyance is written all over my face. "Because I didn't want Mom to have to see you. I figured I'd go out for lunch with you and send you on your way."

"This isn't like you," he says.

"You don't know me anymore," I say.

He leans back into the booth. "I wanted to see you, to get to know you again. It's been too long."

"I'm on Mom's side, in case that isn't obvious." I take an enormous bite of food and then think of something else to say.

"That's fine."

I kind of hate how calm he is. I kind of hate how much I feel like he isn't listening. Like I could say the same thing over and over again and it wouldn't make a dent.

"Here's the thing you don't seem to be understanding: The fact that you haven't seen me in years is all your fault.

I was a child. I don't know why . . ." I feel like I've had this conversation too many times recently. When I had to say the same thing to Paisley, I didn't know what would come of it. I didn't know it would actually lead to something good. But having the same conversation with my dad, I just know that this isn't going to end well. "I don't know why you can't see that. You were the grown-up. I was the child."

He scrubs his hands across his face. "You're really going to hate me when I tell you the next part then."

"What?" I ask. "You want to tell me all about your wonderful family? Show pictures of how great they are?"

"No. Paula and I, we're getting divorced."

"Wow, so sad. I hope you can handle juggling two separate estranged families. I'm sure that will be exhausting for you."

"All right. You know what, Carter? You're obviously going to give me attitude no matter what. I'll stop now."

"Good." I push away my plate even though there's one gorgeous, glistening piece of French toast still sitting there. I don't need his pointless excuses or his French toast.

He pays the check and we leave.

I make him drop me off a block away from the house.

"You realize I've seen your mother multiple times recently. You're not keeping her away from me. You were a child back then, but she's still the grown-up now. She can make her own decisions."

I stare at his face and hate how much he looks like me. Do I have in me the kind of coldness that he has in him?

What if I'm just like him? What if I hurt Paisley? She doesn't deserve that.

I hop out of his truck, shaking with some emotion I can't place. Before I slam the door shut, I say, "See you in another five years."

I go inside and don't look back.

-PAISLEY-

Carter is supposed to pick me up at six o'clock. We were supposed to meet at the mall, but earlier he texted to say he'd pick me up. So here I am standing outside of my condo, actually outside of the complex entirely, so he doesn't get lost on the labyrinth of streets and culs-de-sac. There's a chance that my condo complex is a small Bermuda triangle in the middle of New Jersey. There have been tales of people driving around it and never being heard from again.

I stamp my feet to warm them up. I probably should have put on something warmer than ballet flats. But I liked how they looked with the new T-shirt I made myself. It says "nap it out" in white letters across the front and looks particularly adorable under my bloodred cardigan. I feel like Carter will appreciate this whole look.

But especially the T-shirt.

I should make him one too.

Maybe that's kind of weird? Like to have matching T-shirts with your sort-of boyfriend? Maybe tonight I'll finally get up the nerve to ask him if he's my boyfriend. It shouldn't matter if he is or isn't. But I really want to know anyway. It feels like it's time. I like him so much. I never meant to like him this much.

I hide my face in my hands as if I can hide my embarrassing thoughts.

I've been having these long, circuitous thought tangents for the past two days. Anything to take my mind off what happened on Monday morning.

I feel so bad. With him getting fired like that. I want to make sure that Carter knows how much I appreciate it. That his act of self-sacrifice wasn't lost on me.

I pace a little and text Carter again. I try to call him, but his phone goes straight to voice mail. It's too cold to stay out here. Maybe he got a flat tire. And left his phone at home.

I go back inside and my mom is surprised to see me. Especially since I've been gone for over an hour.

I'm mostly interested in getting the feeling back in my feet and not talking about the fact that I might have been stood up. I want to give Carter the benefit of the doubt, and the best way to do that is to be as vague as possible with my mom.

I don't want her to think less of Carter. I want her to like Carter. Which is an interesting reversal of my feelings, all things considered.

"What happened?" she asked.

"Something came up," I say, the lie coming out easily. "You know, like I said, his mom has been sick."

"Oh no."

"Well, he didn't specifically say that," I say. I'm making excuses and getting nervous, and this is not a great look for me. "I don't have all the details."

"Okay. Well, are you staying home tonight? Maybe we could watch a movie. Hallmark has been playing Christmas stuff for a month already."

I smile but don't commit.

I need to hide in my room for at minimum a half hour. Just be alone and collect my thoughts. Man, it's nice to be alone. I forgot about that. I'm around people literally 24-7 at school, and I forgot how much I value alone time.

I call Carter again, and again it goes right to voice mail.

I should probably get on with my night and assume everything is fine. There's no reason to be nervous. It's a holiday weekend; he probably got trapped hanging out with his family and forgot to bring a charger. He's always playing those weird games on his phone that eat his battery life right up.

I'm sure that's what happened.

I take another deep breath and text Lizzie and Madison.

Paisley: So I think I'm free tonight.

Lizzie: YAY.

Madison: AWESOME.

Paisley: I think Carter is standing me up.

Lizzie: I take back my yay.

Madison: I will cut him.

I laugh and feel a little bit better.

When Madison arrives, she picks me up right in front of my unit so I don't have to stand outside in the cold for long.

"Let's go egg his house," she says by way of greeting.

"Actually," I say, "would you mind taking me to his house? I kind of want to check on him. I'm worried."

She and Lizzie exchange a look but do what I ask.

-CARTER-

I hear a car pull up outside and I know.

I've been sitting in the dark for most of the afternoon and evening. My mom's busy cooking in the kitchen and my sister is out for dinner with some friends from high school. I should probably go in and help my mom, but I'm enjoying my wallow. I don't want to tell her about seeing my dad. I don't want to talk about it.

And I definitely forgot about Paisley.

We were supposed to meet at the mall, but then I decided I would pick her up. It would give me more time to talk to her in the car rather than in the noisy food court.

But then I just didn't.

Over the course of the past couple of hours, I've gotten angrier and angrier with her. I was so worried about hurting her earlier, but then I remembered all the ways she hurt me. Leading right up to me losing my job because of her. And now she's here. Running up to my porch. Like nothing is wrong.

I know how twisted around my thoughts are, that

they're not following any logical order, but I know I can't deal with her. I don't *want* to deal with her. It's better for both of us if I make a clean break now. I'm sure of it.

Just as she's about to ring the doorbell, I slip outside.

She's another thing I don't want my mother to deal with.

"Hey," she says, bright-eyed. She's bouncy, happy, excited. So different from the Paisley I usually see. It should make me feel warm inside; it should be endearing. Instead I'm pissed off that she can't tell that I'm in a bad mood.

"Hey," I say.

She kisses my cheek. "Um, did you forget about me?"

"Yeah, something like that," I say, barely containing my urge to swipe away her kiss.

"What's up? Do you want to come with my high school friends and me to a party?" She gestures over her shoulder at the car parked in front of the house. "I thought maybe you weren't into the mall. So we could do this instead."

She's giving me an out. I could take the out. She'd already forgiven me for standing her up.

"No thanks."

"Just *no thanks*?" she asks with an eyebrow raise.

"I'm not into it."

Her face darkens a bit in the porch light. "What's up? Are you okay? Is it your mom?"

"Nope, I don't want to hang out with your high school friends," I say, my voice sounding nastier than I meant it to.

"Hey, you're the one who stood me up. Is it your dad?"

"Oh my god, Paisley! Stop poking, stop prodding! I don't want to talk about it."

She winces back and away from me, but I can't help it. I don't have any control over this moment.

"I don't want to make excuses. I don't want to explain myself."

"You always say you hate excuses, but there's a difference between reasons and excuses, Carter. Grow up and realize that." Her nose is red from the cold, and I can't feel my feet since I walked out here with only my socks on, but that doesn't stop my face from growing hot with rage.

"Fine, you want to hear some reasons? Here are the reasons I bullied Henry in middle school. My sister left for college, my grandma died, my parents were getting divorced. Suffice to say, it was a hard year. I cried all the time. And then I found out that not only were my parents getting divorced, but also my dad had a secret family, like a wife and a baby. Or not a wife, he wasn't married to her. But whenever he was supposedly traveling for work, he wasn't really traveling for work. He was with them."

She's obviously surprised. And my voice is getting louder and louder.

"But mostly, Paisley, I was a little shit. Only a little shit would act like that, treat someone like Henry that way completely unprovoked. And I don't think I've changed much since then. I don't think you need me around. And I don't think I want to be around you either. Because you're shitty too. We'd end up being shitty to each other." It's like a light bulb going off in my head. The truth of this statement makes my veins buzz with anger.

"What?" She looks so sad I almost take it all back.

"You heard me," I say. "Leave me alone."

"If you would tell me what's wrong. What I did. Maybe I can make it right."

"This isn't about you. Everything isn't about Paisley. Just go away."

She blinks at me, hard, a bunch of times. It's like kicking a puppy but it's better this way. For some reason that eludes me at the moment. But I know it's the way it has to be.

"It seems like it's about me. You just made it about me."

"It's not *just* about you," I amend. And then I go in for the kill. "I don't want to talk to you anymore."

"Fine, Carter. Fine. Whatever you say."

She turns on her heel and leaves.

I head back inside. Rather than going to my room and hiding under the covers, I go into the bright warmth of the kitchen and start peeling potatoes.

I have more important things to deal with than Paisley Turner.

CHAPTER TWENTY-TWO

-PAISLEY-

I ask Lizzie and Madison to bring me home. I can't face the party. And they do it, without question. They don't even make me talk about what happened with Carter. I have a feeling they had the windows open to listen in anyway. I'm sure they were nearly as shocked as I was by what happened.

They exchange several more glances as they drive me home. I imagine that's what it's like to have two parents. Certainly, not anything I would know or understand. I'm sure that's what Carter was thinking when he blew me off.

Because that's all it was. He just blew me off. He had a bad day. There was nothing permanent about this argument.

As I lug myself back up the steps to my home for the second time tonight, I try to imagine what I'm going to tell my mother. I told her I was going to a party with Lizzie and Madison and that I'd be home late. Instead, I'm here. And it's only after nine o'clock. And I'm so embarrassed.

Luckily my mom is dozing on the couch and probably doesn't even realize what time it is.

"Night, Mom," I say.

"Night, sweetheart," she mumbles, rolling over to move closer into the pillows on the sofa.

I take a long shower and try to will myself to cry. I don't cry very easily, but there's a first time for everything. Isn't it supposed to be cathartic?

I have no choice but to go into mourning for the rest of the weekend. I have to go to my grandma's with my mom the next day, but that's easy enough. My aunt is there with her new baby, and everyone's attention is on them. It's almost too easy to hide in the family room and watch whatever's on TV.

The next day, I do even better. I speak to no one. I go so far as to turn my phone off. It feels good knowing that no one can get in touch with me. It's exactly what I need.

-CARTER-

I'm out picking up ice cream on Friday night for Thea because apparently that's what I do now. She had a craving and asked if I'd run out. It's kind of a hard thing to say no to since I barely ever get to drive anymore. And I kind of love to drive. It clears my head.

My head could use some clearing.

I don't exactly know why I freaked out on Paisley the way I did. I don't know how to fix things. I don't know that

I even want to fix things. The fact that I could get so angry, that I could go from zero to sixty just because.

It feels like it has something to do with the fact that she showed up unexpectedly on the same porch that my dad showed up unexpectedly on just a few hours earlier. It was like I needed to punish her for that. But that wasn't Paisley's fault. That was my dad's fault.

I sigh audibly as I pull into the parking lot of the ice cream place. It's in the same strip mall as a Starbucks. There's someone pacing outside of it.

Someone familiar.

Someone, thankfully, not Paisley.

Henry Lai is walking back and forth in front of Starbucks, moving quickly, running his hands through his hair so it sticks straight up.

I approach him slowly. Something's wrong, but I don't know what and it feels like there are too many variables. I don't want to upset him further.

"Hey, Henry," I say as I approach.

He looks over at me, recognition registering on his face. I wonder if he would have recognized me if he hadn't seen me a couple weeks ago. Or if I would have been so far out of context to him that he wouldn't recognize me. Like when Paisley saw me the first night of school and thought I was a stranger.

This isn't about Paisley.

Henry shakes his head at me. "I can't get Paisley to answer her phone."

Except, of course it's about Paisley.

I give him a questioning look. "What?"

He breathes deeply and leans on the brick facade of the building, his hands on his knees.

"There's just some stuff going on and Paisley is the only person who knows about it, but her phone is off or dead or something. And she's not answering. And I need to talk to her."

When I step closer, I can see fine beads of sweat on his forehead. He's trembling all over.

"Are you okay?" I ask.

He shakes his head.

"Are you having a panic attack?"

He nods this time, squeezing his eyes shut.

"Is your car here?"

He shakes his head again. "I walked. I walked really far. I was on the phone and I didn't realize how far I went."

"So something bad happened. You got a phone call that upset you."

"I did," he said, his breath coming in ragged bursts now. "But don't. I don't want to. I don't want to tell you. I need to talk to Paisley."

"Paisley's not answering her phone, remember?"

"Maybe if you call her. Maybe she's tired of talking to me."

I shake my head. "She's not going to answer for me either right now."

He doesn't seem to think it's odd that I know that. I can see his teeth dig into his bottom lip like it's the only way to keep from crying, or howling, or both.

"Can I take you home?" I ask.

"I can't go home. My mom can't see me like this. She can't know what was going on. I don't know where to go. I need to talk to Paisley."

Of course he does. I think of a million other things to do with Henry. I could stick him in an Uber. Or drive him somewhere besides home. I could take him back to my house.

"All right. I'll take you to Paisley." I haven't forgotten about Thea's ice cream, so I shoot her a text that it's going to take a few extra minutes.

Thea: It better not melt on the way home!

Carter: It's thirty degrees out. I'm sure it'll be fine.

I help Henry get settled in the passenger seat. He radiates cold, like he's nearly frozen through in his light jacket. He must have been outside for an awfully long time.

"She didn't answer," Henry repeats in the car, staring out the window.

"Paisley?" I ask, but I don't even wait for him to respond. "That's probably more my fault than yours. I think she might have her phone off. We had a fight." Or maybe I'm giving myself too much credit. Maybe her phone is dead or on silent. Maybe she's at the movies.

Maybe Paisley has already gone back to being aloof, emotionless Paisley. That'd be better for everyone involved. Though it's super dick of her not to be answering Henry.

That doesn't seem like her. She's never been that aloof. Henry has always been her soft spot.

Henry gives me stuttered directions on how to get to Paisley's house, and I can't help thinking about how I was supposed to meet her there the other night. That was my fault. But somehow it feels like hers.

When Henry tells me which building is Paisley's, I pull up out front. He struggles with the seat belt and then the door handle, and I realize I should probably help him. I really don't want to see Paisley, but I also don't want to see Henry fall on his ass. His legs are like Jell-O.

I make sure he doesn't fall but I also don't touch him. I know that people having panic attacks don't always like to be touched, and I don't want to make this any harder on Henry than it already is.

I knock on the door.

I wait for Paisley, but instead her mom answers. "Hey, guys," she says. And then she calls over her shoulder. "Paisley, Henry and some other boy are here."

-PAISLEY-

Henry and some other boy are here.

I can't even imagine who this other boy would be. Who would Henry drag to my house unannounced? But when I see Henry, I know he's not exactly in his right mind.

"Henry," I say, putting my hand on his arm. He's obviously upset. And then I see Carter. "What the hell did you do?"

"Are you kidding me, Paisley? I didn't do anything. I brought him over here because I found him like this at Starbucks and he said he couldn't go home, that he wanted to see you."

Henry hangs his head.

"Do you need a hug?" Paisley asks.

Henry shakes his head. "Some water'd be good," he says.

Henry makes his way into the condo and I want to invite Carter in. I want everything to be normal with us, even though I know it's not.

He's about to turn away, but I can't let him go that easily.

"So you do know where I live," I say.

"I could figure it out. I just didn't want to see you the other night," he says, his voice as cold as the air around us.

"Which would be why you treated me like a pariah when I showed up at your house." I hug myself to ward off the cold but I'm only in thin pajamas so it's not really working.

"I didn't invite you there," he says.

"I don't get you, Carter."

"What's to get? I made a mistake getting involved with you. You never cared about me. You never will care about me."

"I'm so confused. What happened?"

"Nothing."

"What did I do?"

"For god's sake, Paisley, I told you this wasn't about you. This has nothing to do with you. I don't want to see you anymore."

"I feel like you're giving me a lot of mixed messages, not least of which is showing up at my house like this."

"I'm here because I found your best friend mid-panic attack and didn't want to leave him out in the elements."

"That was nice of you. But you're always nice."

"Gee, thanks," he says, sarcasm dripping from his words. "Maybe you could have noticed that sooner before you tried to sabotage my whole life."

"I thought we were past that? I thought we were good? We made out every night for a week. I thought we were moving toward something."

"Maybe we were. Maybe we were just making out. But I realized it's not worth it. I don't think it's worth the trouble. We'll have the same problems in different ways."

"And we can't at least try?"

"It'll be a lot of bullshit and excuses."

"I don't understand what your issue with excuses is. You're allowed to have reasons behind the things you do."

"Well," he says, obviously defeated. Obviously leaving for real this time. "Maybe I know you won't like any of mine."

And just like that he's gone.

I have bigger things to deal with, though.

I go inside and find Henry sitting on my bed, nursing a glass of water. I sit next to him.

"Are you okay? What's happening?"

"Jana called. She says we need to end it or go to our professor. That she's not comfortable continuing, especially since she's the one who will be grading my final exam."

"Well, it's better to end it than have her tell the professor, right?"

He shakes his head. "I'm pretty sure I'm in love with her."

I put my arm around his shoulders and he slumps into me. "I'm sorry. That's the worst."

"It really, really is."

I rub his arm. "I'm sorry I didn't answer your call. I had my phone off."

He looks at me curiously.

"Carter troubles. Lots of Carter troubles."

"I'm not shocked, but on the other hand, I kind of am. He's a good guy. Better than expected," Henry says.

"Well, he's not our problem anymore. He doesn't want anything to do with me."

"What did you do?" he asks.

"Me? Nothing! I didn't do anything."

I fill him in on what happened at work.

"Well, the moral high ground would be you confessing to your part in the firing. Maybe that would put you on even ground."

"Maybe. But he acted like that wasn't necessary," I insist. But the more I insist, the more I wonder.

"Maybe he decided it was."

"Maybe he could tell me these things."

"Maybe."

"Let's forget our relationship troubles and watch something nerdy," Henry suggests.

"Best idea I've heard all day," I tell him.

CHAPTER TWENTY-THREE

-CARTER-

"How was your weekend?" Ray asks when I get back to school Sunday afternoon. He's playing some game on his computer and asks if I want to join. Which I do, even though what I should be doing is studying for finals.

"Complete and utter shit," I say, dragging over my desk chair and slumping into it.

He pauses the game. "Is the cancer back? You should have texted me."

"Nope, no bad news with my mom," I say. Then I fill him in on not only losing my job, which we hadn't had a chance to talk about last week, but also having to deal with my dad and having two separate fights with Paisley.

"Wow. That's freaking exhausting. I am exhausted on your behalf."

"At least I know I'm not being too dramatic about it."

"What are you going to do?"

"Such a good question that I've been trying to answer," I say. "The job, I'm not sure there's anything I can do. I sacrificed myself for the greater good and it was a fireable offense either way. I just wanted to save Paisley. In hindsight, that was not my smartest move ever."

"Dude, forget Paisley. She messed everything up. That was super not cool of her to do. Maybe if you hadn't had those two strikes already they wouldn't have come down so hard on you. She needs to tell them about what happened."

"But those strikes, they happened before," I say, wanting to defend her mostly out of habit, I suppose.

"Before what? Before you were a human? Who does shit like that to begin with? I'll never forgive her for stealing my birthday leftovers anyway." He unpauses the game and we take our frustrations out on the fake bad guys on the screen.

"She's not a villain," I say, but I'm laughing now. It's nice to feel like Ray is on my side of this. "And we got back at her for that. Between the duct-taped door and, you know, ruining her T-shirt business."

Ray scoffs. "She did terrible shit to you. You don't have to take it just because you like her. Because you're a masochist."

I shake my head. "I liked her for a long time when we were younger. She was my first real crush. I never expected to see her here. So when I did, it felt like destiny. Like we were destined to be together. And she felt worth fighting for. I can't believe how wrong I was in so many ways."

"She's not worth your time," he says. "So what's the deal with your dad?"

She might have been worth my time if I hadn't gone off on her the other night. But I keep that thought to myself.

"If Paisley's not worth my time, then he definitely isn't," I say as I take out another big boss on the screen. Playing video games while fueled by rage seems to be really good for me.

"Well, you had a way worse weekend than me. I was annoyed by my nonstop family time and the fact that my dad got mad at my mom for not making this one corn dish he likes. But then she made it for him on Saturday and everything was okay."

"Oh, to have your problems," I say.

"I know. It's a good life."

I grin at him. We take out the next boss and things feel better.

Talking to Ray definitely helped.

-PAISLEY-

It's a week after we got back from Thanksgiving and finals are already upon us.

After way too many sleepless nights, I decide I need to confess my sins to Jordan. If Carter got fired for making out at work, it's only fair that I do too.

Jordan is working today at least, and I track her down in the supply room, better known at the ball closet because, literally, it's where we store all variety of balls. We're not very clever, but we have fun.

She's leaning over a large rubber tub. I can't see what's

in there, but she seems to be sorting into some smaller buckets around her.

"Hey, Paisley," she says when she sees me. "You're not on the schedule today."

"No. I know."

Then she turns to look at me fully. "Are you okay?"

I know I look like utter shit. I'm wearing the pajamas I've slept in for the past three nights and I haven't washed my hair in who knows how long. The bags under my eyes are dark and deep.

"Are you sick?"

"No, no," I say. "I need to tell you something. Do you have a minute to talk?"

"I do if you're willing to help me sort through these," she says. She tips the tub toward me. It's a complicated mess of tennis balls, Ping-Pong balls, racket balls, and handballs.

"How did this happen?" I ask.

"Laziness," she says. I settle next to her but not too close. Lord knows what I smell like at this point.

"So, have exams gotten the better of you?"

I nod. "And there's something else."

"Is it about Carter?'

"Yes."

"I know he's your buddy, but he was on his third strike. And it doesn't even matter because he was definitely not supposed to be engaging in such behavior on the job."

"Well, the thing is," I say, still half wincing at the use of the word *buddy*. He was so much more than my buddy. "It was my fault."

"How do you figure?" she asks, pulling out a Wiffle

ball and examining it. "I didn't even know we had Wiffle balls," she mutters, tossing it into a separate bucket behind her.

"I was the girl who was under the desk with him," I say. "I came to see him at work even though I wasn't on the clock. And I'm the one who engaged with him even though there technically was no kissing."

"Wait, seriously? There was no kissing?"

I shake my head. "We were under the desk because I dropped a pen. And then I had to take my cardigan off because it got snagged on something. So we probably looked like we're in a compromising position, when really it was just a weird moment to be caught during."

Jordan nods, her face dark with thought, so I continue.

"Those early strikes of Carter's, they were my fault. I did a whole bunch of things like that to him. I was messing with him. I didn't like him because he was mean to my friend in middle school."

"You and Carter have known each other since middle school?" she asks, a delighted smile crossing her face. "No wonder you're so easy together."

"Jordan. It's all my fault. I was playing pranks on him, and they all got out of hand. I acted like I didn't know where he was even though he told me he was going to office hours. The dye in the hand sanitizer was aimed at me because I'd been pranking him and that was his revenge."

Now I have her attention. "Why would you do those things?"

I shrug. "Because I was mad at him. I thought I could teach him a lesson. I wanted to make him miserable."

She pushes away from the ball bin and shakes her head. "This is not great news, Paisley."

I nod.

"Why didn't he say anything?"

"Because he's Carter. He hates excuses. He hates having to explain himself. It's not his way of doing things."

She rubs her temples. "It seems like you two have had a pretty rough semester."

"Carter's was a lot rougher than mine."

"I'm going to reconsider my 'three strikes and you're out' policy. Just this once. And I'm going to talk to Mr. Martell. I'll explain to him what happened. That he got the wrong idea but you guys knew there wasn't a good way to explain it."

I nod vigorously.

"I'll give you both a clean slate in January."

"I can keep my job?"

She nods.

"What? Really? Why?"

She shrugs. "Because I've been here a long time and you guys are great. You're helpful and punctual. Even with the terrible early shifts we've given you."

"I don't think he's going to want to work with me," I say, realization dawning.

"We'll cross that bridge when we get to it. I'll let Carter know that he has his job back." Jordan stands and brushes off her pants. The closet organizing isn't done, but I guess she has bigger things to deal with right now.

"Wait," I say, standing up. "Can I tell him? Can you

give me a little time before you call him? He probably never wants to talk to me again, but I can at least tell him the good news before he shuns me forever."

"Yeah, sure," she says.

"Thanks, Jordan."

Now I'm a woman on a mission.

My heart soars at the possibilities.

-CARTER-

Carter: Things are really bad.

Thea: What? What's wrong?

Carter: Everything is really bad.

Thea: How/why? Is it Dad? Did something happen?

Carter: No. It's Paisley. I didn't want to talk about it over the weekend, but I got fired from my job last week. It was a little bit her fault, and a little bit mine. But I took the fall. Then I stood her up the other day because, well, I don't really know why. I couldn't bear to see her. So then, on top of that, I picked a fight with her. And now I don't know what to do.

Thea: My god. She got you fired? What a little bitch.

Carter: She didn't get me fired. Chill out. It was both of us. Something happened at work that looked worse than it was.

Thea: Still. How dare she?

Carter: Thea, listen. I messed up. I'm the one who turned it all upside down.

Thea: Why?

Carter: I wanted to push her away. Even though I like her.

Thea: Do you really like her?

Carter: Yeah.

Thea: I don't get it.

Carter: She's funny. She's always on time. She works hard. She really cares about things. She overcompensates sometimes, but that just makes her a better friend.

Thea: So you really like her.

Carter: I do. I needed someone to talk to, even though I'm still mad at you about making me see Dad.

Thea: Yeah, I know. I just didn't want you to regret not hanging out with him.

Carter: I know. I know.

Thea: But listen. You don't need the drama in your life. I know girls like Paisley. They never seem to know what they want. If you really like her, give her some time. Maybe she's going through a bad phase. Or maybe she'll grow out of it. Or maybe this is who she is.

Carter: Maybe.

Thea: But you don't have to let her take you down with her.

Carter: You know how you didn't want me to regret anything with Dad? Well, I don't want to regret anything with Paisley.

Thea: I'm not sure that's exactly the

same thing, but I understand what you're
getting at.

Carter: Things were so good between us
for a little while. I want to get back
to that. But I'm having trouble forgiv-
ing her for getting me fired AND for not
confessing that she was involved. But
it's not fair, because I told her I'd
take care of it.

Thea: Does she know you want her to
confess?

Carter: No. I want her to know to do that.

Thea: Well, she's not a mind reader. But
on the other hand, she might not be the
person you want her to be. Sometimes
that's how life is.

Carter: I know. I don't want to be disappointed in her.

Thea: You're allowed to protect yourself. You don't have to jump through
hoops for this girl.

Carter: Who said anything about jump-
ing through hoops?

Thea: Fine. Fine.

Carter: Thanks for listening.

Thea: You're welcome. Don't get yourself all tied up in knots over some girl.

Carter: She's not just some girl.

Thea: If you really think that, then maybe she's worth the hoops.

Carter: Yeah. I need to think about this for a while.

Thea: Good luck.

Carter: Thanks again.

-PAISLEY-

I find Carter alone in his room, staring at an open book on his desk. We have our calc exam tomorrow and I'm definitely not prepared. I hope he is.

I'm still a mess. I didn't even let myself take a shower before I went looking for him. Luckily, I didn't have to cast a wide net since we live in the same dorm.

I knock lightly on the doorjamb.

He looks over at me but doesn't say anything.

"Can I come in?" I ask.

"Sure, whatever," he says, slamming his book shut. He unlocks his phone, looks at the screen for a second, and then flips it over. As if he needs to make absolutely sure that I won't be able to read anything on it.

"So," I say. I sit in Ray's desk chair and Carter turns his body to face me.

"So. What's up? I have an exam tomorrow and I'm not speaking to my calc tutor," he says.

I gulp. "I got your job back."

"You what?"

"I got your job back. I went to Jordan and I told her I was involved. In everything. Every time you messed up, I was behind it. I explained that we weren't even really kissing under the desk, and she believed me."

"You really did that?" he asks, his face softening almost imperceptibly.

I nod.

He nods and stares at the floor.

"I just wanted to tell you the good news."

He doesn't respond.

"I could help you with calc," I offer.

"Thanks, I'll let you know."

"Okay. Well, Jordan will call you soon."

"Sure, whatever. Can you close the door on your way out?"

I do. I stand in the hallway outside of his room for a second to catch my breath. I have work to do. I have a shower to take. And I'm in need of a nap.

At least I finally did the right thing.

I go back to the room, intent on studying, but all I can think about is how dirty my hair is. I take a shower, luxuriating in the hot water and then go back to the room where I put on the fluffiest and most comfortable clothes I own and get back to studying.

I probably shouldn't flunk out of school on top of everything else.

As I'm about to get back to studying, Stef comes in.

"Hey," she says.

"Hi."

"You took a shower. How fun for us."

"Yeah. I'm sorry about that. I didn't mean to wait so long. I'm just . . ."

"Exhausted? Sad? Anxious? Completely wrung out?"

"All of the above?"

She grins.

"I'm really sorry," I say. "About, you know, everything."

"I'm sorry too."

"No way," I say. Uncurling from the corner of my bed. "I messed up so much more than you did. All I could think about was Carter."

"I was being touchy about relationship stuff since nothing worked out with Melissa. It was hard to watch you be happy with Carter who you pretty much hated this whole semester and somehow ended up in a relationship with."

"We weren't really in a relationship. We were just . . . making out."

"But still, I'm sorry I wasn't there for you. And that I was taking things out on you. That's not fair. At all."

"I like you enough that I don't mind being your punching bag sometimes," I say with a shrug.

"Back at you," she says.

We stand in the middle of our room and hug, squeezing each other, like if we hug tightly enough maybe we can forget all the bad.

For a minute it works. Everything terrible in the world feels just a little bit further away.

"I also, kind of, sort of have a date."

"With Melissa?" I ask.

"With a girl from my psych class." She smiles so wide I can't help but smile with her.

"That's awesome."

"It is," she agrees. "There are always other fish, Paisley."

"There are," I say.

"I guess we should study," Stef says with a sigh.

Just like that, the terrible comes crashing back in. But at least things are okay with Stef. At least I got Carter's job back.

At least I'll be able to sleep tonight.

CHAPTER TWENTY-FOUR

-CARTER-

Sleep is good.

I like sleep way more than I remembered.

I let myself sleep almost a whole day after my last exam. My mom and Thea pick me up the next morning, and I take home whatever I need for my nearly month's long vacation. I look around the room, making sure I'm not forgetting anything.

When I get home, I watch a lot of TV, not even caring what's on.

I think about maybe texting Paisley, but I think that might be a bad idea. I'm not completely sure that I'm ready for her. I will be, though. Because I miss her. I miss her a lot more than I could have expected. And she did make things right in the end. Through her own Paisley brand of justice, I suppose.

The second day of break, I force myself to put on real

clothes and I go to the mall. I really need to buy my mom a Christmas present. I don't find anything.

When I get home from my failed shopping trip, there are two pieces of mail waiting for me. One is a package with a familiar return address and the other is a smaller envelope with an unfamiliar return address.

I open the envelope first, since that's the wild card.

It's a handwritten note from my dad with tickets to the aquarium.

Carter—

I know I messed up. And I'm sorry. I'm not going to give you a long lecture about how I deserve to be in your life, but I'd at least like you to consider it.

I'd like to take you the aquarium. Just as a first step. If you don't want to go with me, take someone else, but at least have fun.

Sometimes saying I'm sorry is the hardest thing you can do, but I know how hard accepting apologies can be too. I want you to know that I'm trying and that if you meet me halfway I'll do my best to never let you down again.

Love, Dad

I want to be angry with him, but it's hard to hate someone in the face of tickets to the aquarium. Maybe it's time to try again. I'm older. I'm more prepared to be disappointed.

I could always meet him there, so even if he ditches me (again) I'd still get to spend a day at the aquarium. It'd be a win-win situation. Even more than that, it'd give him the chance to prove me right all over again.

But wouldn't it be nice if he could prove me wrong?

I slide the envelope into my back pocket. I need to think about that a little more.

When I open the package, I find a T-shirt with the words I'M SORRY emblazoned on the front and a sad face emoji on the back.

Thea walks in as I'm examining it.

I hold it up for her. "It's from Paisley."

"Oh, that's . . . That's sweet. Kind of weird, but sweet."

"She makes T-shirts. She screen-prints them herself. It's, like, her hobby."

"Less weird. Still sweet. Also, still a little weird."

"Are you experiencing some kind of malfunction wherein the only words you know are *sweet* and *weird*?"

"Weirdly sweet, sweetly weird," Thea says, nodding.

"That's a really good description of Paisley, honestly."

"So what are you going to do?" Thea asks.

"I want to see her. I miss her. Maybe we could have a fresh start." If I'm thinking about giving my dad a second chance, there's no reason not to do the same for Paisley. After that day she came to tell me she got my job back, I wanted to talk to her, I wanted to say more. But my brain was muddled and exams were busy. It was all too much. I wasn't going to be my best self.

"Sounds good."

"I don't know if I trust her," I say, leaning my hip on the kitchen counter and squeezing the T-shirt in my hands. I'm glad Thea doesn't know about what my dad sent me, because I don't want to talk about that. But I do want to talk about Paisley.

"Or myself," I add as an afterthought. "I get so angry sometimes."

"Well, I don't know what to tell you."

"So, no advice?"

"None."

"But I need advice."

"It seems like I've given you lots of advice over the past few months, and I have a feeling it wasn't always the kind you needed. I'm going to leave you to your own devices on this one," she says, breezing out of the kitchen.

There's got to be someone who can give me some advice, someone who knows Paisley well enough to help. I pick up my phone and send a text.

-PAISLEY-

What I want to do when the semester is over is sleep for a week. Exams are exhausting. I feel like no one warned me about how exhausting they would be.

Obviously, it wasn't helpful that I was also going through one of the most emotionally stressful times of my life. But whatever.

I didn't see Carter again after that afternoon in his room, minus a few run-ins at exams. But I didn't even try to talk to him. I didn't have the bandwidth to deal with him and exams.

Maybe I'll send him a text over the break, maybe I won't.

Maybe he'll send me a text, once he gets my apology T-shirt. The post office said it might take up to a week for it to get to him this time of year, but at least it'll get there. At least he'll know I thought of him.

I spend the first couple of days of winter break at home in my pajamas. I start working again at my high school job. The turnover rate in the mall food court is pretty high, so my old boss wants me back even if it's only for a couple of weeks. At least he won't have to train me.

After a long shift at the potato stand on Christmas Eve Eve, I head over to Henry's. We're snuggled up in his basement TV room watching *The Last Jedi*.

"Who are you texting?" I ask when Henry's screen lights up for the millionth time in the past hour.

"No one," he says.

"If it's Amelia Vaughn, I'm not helping you again this time."

"It's not Amelia Vaughn."

"Is it some other girl?" I ask, raising my eyebrows. "Is it Jana? Are things working out between you two?"

"Actually," he starts.

I pause the movie, waiting for more explanation and really hoping that maybe he's worked things out with her.

"I've been kind of talking to this girl who works at the reserves desk in the engineering building."

"Oooh la la!" I say. "I can't believe you haven't told me about her. The reserves desk girl and your calc TA. Are you juggling two women?"

"I'm not juggling two women. Jana and I are taking a big step back. Mostly because she says I'm young and inexperienced. Which I am. The reserves desk girl, Laila, her name is, she's, I don't know. We only talk when I'm there. But maybe something can happen."

"Laila Lai? Doesn't have the best ring to it. I'd tell her to keep her own last name, but aside from that, I'm sure you'll be perfect together."

"We're not getting married." Henry rolls his eyes. "And I can't believe that you would imply that a woman would have to take my last name if we did."

It's my turn to roll my eyes. "I'm teasing you, Henry."

"Fine. But we're nothing."

"But you've been texting her all night," I point out.

"Oh no," he says, shaking his head and giving me a patented no-nonsense Henry look. "This isn't Laila."

"You're driving me up the wall. Who. Are. You. Talking. To."

I grab for his phone and he dives to pull it away, but I'm too fast. My reflexes are too much for him. I look at the screen as another text pops up.

"You sure?" the latest text says.

And it's from Carter.

My Carter.

"You're texting Carter?"

"Yes," Henry says, grabbing his phone back and typing a message.

"Why?"

"Well, he might be coming over."

"What? I have to leave."

"He's not coming over to see me, Paisley," Henry says.

I grab my coat, but I can't find one of my gloves; it seems to have fallen out of the pocket. "Is this an ambush?"

"Maybe more like an intervention."

"What? Why are you being so coy? I need real answers."

Henry explains how Carter texted him earlier, hoping that Henry could give him some advice about me. And Henry obliged, because Henry is the best.

"Thank you," I say.

"I didn't love doing this. Mostly because ew, emotions. But you needed some help."

"I did. Especially since emotions are the worst."

Henry's phone lights up again.

"He's outside."

"Are you coming?"

"Definitely not."

"Keep the movie paused?"

"Nah. I think we can continue some other time. You need to talk to Carter. Don't worry about me."

I leave through the basement door. I look up at the sky. It's supposed to snow tonight, so the stars are all covered in clouds.

I take a deep breath and close my eyes, imagining a moonlit sky peppered with stars.

I make a wish and hope that there's a star out there somewhere to grant it.

It's starting to snow as Paisley comes around the side of the house. She's all bundled up in a ski jacket that I've never seen her wear before. She has a hat and gloves on, and I realize she's way more prepared for the weather than I am.

I didn't know it was going to snow or I would have put on a warmer jacket.

It's really cold out.

"Carter?" she asks, her confused voice floating across the street.

And then she's right in front of me. I forget all about the cold. I feel warmer than I have in weeks just because she's standing there.

"I got your package," I say.

"Oh cool. You could have texted me about it. You didn't have to come here."

"I wanted to see you," I say.

"I wanted to see you too. But I thought"—she pauses and shakes her head—"I thought I ruined everything. I'm so sorry if I ruined everything. I never meant to be a ruiner. I got in over my head in every possible way."

I shrug. "It happens. Sometimes it just happens. I got in over my head too. I don't really know how to share? Like, emotionally."

"Well, I'm still sorry. Like, really sorry. I never meant to hurt you."

"I never meant to hurt you either."

"Well, in the interest of honesty. I did mean to hurt you,

sometimes. Like back in September. Back then. But I never meant to *really* hurt you. I never meant to ruin you."

"You didn't ruin me."

"I certainly tried," she says, her tone earnest.

"You didn't deserve the things I said to you at Thanksgiving. I was, well, I had a lot going on. And I guess instead of telling you and letting you in, I pushed you away. That wasn't cool." It feels like my mouth is full of marbles. I expect her to say something, ask me questions, have a big talk about everything we each did wrong. But I can never predict Paisley.

"So why are you here? Not that I'm not thrilled to see you."

"It's Christmas Eve Eve and I wanted to give you this." I hand her the poorly wrapped box that I'm holding.

She grins. "Did you wrap this yourself?"

"How could you tell?"

I shiver.

"We could sit in the car," she says. "If you're too cold."

"In a minute. I want to see you right in front of me a little longer."

She gives me a confused look and then opens the box, pulling out a red T-shirt.

CAN WE KETCHUP SOMETIME? it reads.

She laughs. She laughs so hard she drops the box and the wrapping paper. The wind picks them up and blows them around the street.

We both chase after the debris, trying to catch the quickly scattering paper.

A minute later, we have everything and the snow is coming down harder.

"Let's get in the car," I say.

She follows me and slides into the passenger seat. I dump the box and the paper in the back and stare at her.

"So I was hoping we could try again," I say, after we're quiet for a few minutes. I don't know what she's thinking, but I can't take the silence.

"Really?" she asks.

"Yeah," I say.

"I have to ask, where did you get the T-shirt on such short notice?"

"Oh, well, I actually had it made a while ago."

"Seriously?"

"Yeah, I thought it'd be a good Christmas present."

"It's perfect." She looks back over at me. "So when are we going to get back to trying again?"

"Maybe now?"

I smile.

"I think now is as good a time as any," she says, leaning over the center console. "You never fail to surprise me."

"Right back at you," I say.

And we kiss. It's even better than the first time. Better than the second time, third time, fourth time. I don't even know how that's possible. Maybe it's the relief mixed in with everything else. But it's a damn good kiss.

"Listen," I say, pulling away. "I need a favor from you."

"Anything."

"I know it's eight o'clock on Christmas Eve Eve, but I

haven't found a present for my mom yet. Any chance you'd be willing to brave the mall and help me?"

"If it was anyone else, I'd say no. But for you?"

"Also no?"

She laughs. "For you, I'll make an exception."

"You're too good to me."

"I thought we already established that I'm really not," she says.

I put the car into drive.

"You're perfect to me," I say, threading our fingers together.

And I mean it.

"Right back at you," she says with a grin.

ACKNOWLEDGMENTS

As usual, top billing must go to my wonderful editor, Holly West. Her patience, guidance, enthusiasm, and kindness are always top-notch. I wouldn't be publishing my fifth book without her. Many thanks to Lauren Scobell, who mentioned that she thought I should try my hand at an "enemies to lovers" book (she was right) and to Emily Settle for always being so helpful. I'd also like to thank Andre-Naquian Wheeler, who read a late draft of this book and came up with so many ways to make it stronger.

Big thanks to my favorite draft reader, Lauren Velella. And even bigger thanks to Jennifer Honeybourn and Natalie Williams for each reading a draft and giving such incredibly useful feedback. I'm a better writer because of my writing friends.

Sometimes I'll have conversations that really shape a story, and this book was no different. Michelle Petrasek listened to me babble about the plot at the very beginning of the process and Karole Cozzo listened to me toward the very end. Without those two conversations the whole shape of the story would be different.

I couldn't do any of this without the love and support of my family, especially my mom, Pat. Thanks for everything, Mom.

Check out more books chosen for publication by readers like you.

READER
Swoon
READS
APPROVED

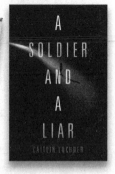

DID YOU KNOW...

READER
Swoon
READS
APPROVED

readers like you
helped to get this
book published?

Join our book-obsessed community and help us
discover awesome new writing talent.

1 Write it.
Share your original YA manuscript.

2 Read it.
Discover bright new bookish talent.

3 Share it.
Discuss, rate, and share your faves.

4 Love it.
Help us publish the books you love.

Share your own manuscript or dive between the pages
at **swoonreads.com** or by downloading the **Swoon Reads app.**